THE [illegible]

Born in New York City, [illegible] Windsor has worked as a dancer, freelance artist, editor and teacher, as well as an author of young adult novels (one of which, *The Sandman's Eyes*, won the Edgar Allen Poe Award from the Mystery Writers of America).

She now lives in Savannah, Georgia.

Also by Patricia Windsor in Pan Macmillan

The Hero
The Sandman's Eyes
Just Like the Movies

The Dream Killer

Patricia Windsor

PAN

First published in USA 1991 by Scholastic Inc

This Pan edition published in Great Britain 1992 by
PAN MACMILLAN CHILDREN'S BOOKS
a division of Pan Macmillan Publishers Limited
Cavaye Place London SW10 9PG
and Basingstoke

Associated companies throughout the world

ISBN 0-330-32502-7

9 8 7 6 5 4 3 2 1

A CIP catalogue record for this book is available from
the British Library

Printed in England by Clays Ltd, St Ives plc

To my good friends E.W. Count and Milton Wyatt

Part One

Rose

One

NANCY EMERSON DISAPPEARED THE WEDNESDAY before Thanksgiving. She'd been baby-sitting at the Berrys' and left to walk home just after dark. Around seven-thirty, her mother phoned to ask if Nancy would be back in time for supper. Mrs. Berry was surprised; Nancy had been gone for more than two hours. Nancy's mother remembered her daughter saying she wanted to meet some friends at the mall that evening. Uneasily, Mrs. Emerson waited until nine o'clock when everyone had returned home. Nobody had seen Nancy. Something was very wrong. Mrs. Emerson called Silver Henning, the police chief. A search party was organized. It was out all night but Nancy wasn't found.

The Thanksgiving atmosphere was tainted. Although people were worried, they also seemed annoyed, as if Nancy could have picked a better time to disappear.

Rose Potter remembered the previous winter

when she'd actually spoken to Nancy. It seemed strange now, but maybe that was only hindsight.

It had been a cold and dreary day, the kind Rose liked to think of as Thomas Hardy weather, complete with leaden sky and ashen leaves. The kind of day poets made into romantic melancholy but which often left her feeling just plain grumpy. She had been walking home from dance class, willing herself not to shiver as the sweat turned to ice crystals on her back. She'd been too lazy to change properly and had just thrown her parka over her thin, damp leotard. Rose was busy hypnotizing herself into being warm, saying it like a mantra over and over in her head. She crashed right into Nancy Emerson.

Nancy began apologizing before Rose could get a word out. Her nose was running, and her eyes were red.

"No, it was my fault," Rose said, but Nancy burst into tears and made no effort to brush them away as they rolled down her face.

"It's not that," she said, sniffing.

Rose waited a moment out of politeness. There didn't seem much point in hanging around. But when Rose turned to go, Nancy grabbed her arm. "I'm in trouble," she said. "I don't know what to do."

It was one of those moments when you have to decide whether to be virtuous or your usual selfish self. Rose felt around in her duffel for a dingy tissue and made some sympathetic noises.

"This is really stupid," Nancy said after she'd blown her nose.

"It's okay."

"I've just got to face it."

"Face what?"

Nancy looked up. She was short and pudgy, with the kind of very white skin that comes out in red spots in the cold. Her blonde hair was straggly and her eyes puffy but she was cute in spite of it, like a cuddly piglet in her pink down jacket.

"You're the Cleer girl, aren't you?" she asked. "Rose?"

Rose nodded. It wasn't the time to get into explanations about her name being Rosecleer, an obsolete name that had somehow appealed to her mother.

"Look," she said to Nancy, "I don't know what your problem is, but I'm freezing. Want to come over to my house for hot chocolate?"

Nancy nodded gratefully and came tagging along, still sniffling.

"You a cheerleader?" she asked, eyeing the big duffel that was full of Rose's dance gear. Rose laughed and said no, she wasn't the cheerleader type. Nancy confided her hopes of getting on the team. "I may not make it, 'cause I'm so short," she said. "But I'm gonna try hard."

Something changed inside Rose then; a subtle shifting of the heart. Suddenly Nancy was a real person, not a cute piglet. Rose slowed down for her to catch up. They walked along companionably for a bit and then Nancy stopped.

"I feel a lot better now." She swiped at her nose with the ragged tissue. "Thanks."

"But I didn't do anything," Rose protested.

Nancy shook her head under the street lamp,

and its golden light caught the tears clinging to her eyelashes, making them sparkle.

"Yeah, you did. Listen, I can't come to your house. I have to go. Thanks for asking me, though." She gave a watery smile and backed away. "Thanks a lot."

"Really . . . it was nothing. . . ." Rose said, bewildered, but Nancy had turned and was trotting down the dark street on her chubby legs. Poor piglet, Rose thought, you'll never be a cheerleader, and she felt a flash of anger at Doreen, the cheering squad captain. Doreen's skinny legs were at least forty feet long, and everyone on the team was chosen to match.

She went home and took a hot bath and never gave another thought to Nancy Emerson or whatever her problem was. Nancy was two years behind Rose in school anyway. Their paths didn't cross. After a while, it was as if that wintry meeting had never happened.

The Potters said a prayer for her over the turkey and stuffing and cranberry sauce, and all ate too much, as usual, and fell asleep in front of the football game on TV. Rose woke with a fuzzy head and dry mouth. Her dad was snoring. Her brother Jerram was simultaneously watching the game, reading a book and doing his math homework. Mom was in the kitchen, washing out the roasting pan. The house still had the Thanksgiving smell, nice but a little greasy. When Rose walked into the kitchen, her mother asked if she wanted a hot turkey sandwich.

"You've got to be kidding."

"You'll all be hungry again later. Just when I've got all the leftovers nicely arranged in their containers and the kitchen is spotless, you'll all be in here for another meal."

She looked so cosily motherly at that moment, wearing her yellow plastic apron over her good dress, her face all satisfied with having Thanksgiving almost over. Rose hugged her.

"I was thinking about that girl," she said, hugging back.

Rose almost said "Me, too," but in truth she hadn't given Nancy a thought since dinner.

"It must be terrible for her parents. Not knowing is worse than knowing the worst," Mom said.

They stood with their arms around each other, their reflections safe and sound in the window over the kitchen sink.

By eight-thirty, everybody did want hot turkey sandwiches. Jerram ate his with his earphones on, tapping on the kitchen table so it shook and fiddling with his calculator.

Dad announced he was going to spend the entire weekend on the couch.

"You always say that, Carl," Mom said. "But you never sit down for a minute."

"I've been sitting down all afternoon, and I'll still be sitting come Sunday night. That's a promise."

"We'll see," Mom said smugly.

And she was right. They called on Friday morning to ask Dad to join the search for Nancy. The sky was like lead. Snow threatened. Rose watched him zip up his jacket in the back hall. He looked grim.

"I'm coming, too," Rose said impulsively.

"No, darlin'. You don't want to be there if we find her."

"You think it's bad as that?"

He gave her a flat look, like he didn't really want to think about it, no less speak. Jerram came rushing downstairs in the ratty sweats he slept in. "Wait up, I'm coming," he shouted and ran back to get dressed.

"Me, too," Rose insisted but made no move toward her coat.

Mom stood in the kitchen doorway, her arms wrapped around herself, still in her raspberry-red robe.

"You don't have to go, too, Jerram," she said when he came back down to put on his boots.

Jerram straightened, red in the face from his efforts at doing up his Velcro straps. "I've never seen a dead body," he said.

Mom looked stricken. "Don't say that, we don't know . . ."

"No more discussion, please," Dad said. "Let's just get this over with."

When they opened the door a harsh wind blew in. Rose shivered and changed her mind about going. She went upstairs to sit in her big old favorite chair and glare out the window at the sky and hope for snow or sun . . . something to make the season seem alive.

The search was unsuccessful that day and the next. On Sunday, there was a silent prayer for

Nancy in church. The atmosphere was morbid. Rose felt her mother's hand grab hers. She wondered if her mother was feeling glad that it wasn't Rose who had disappeared. And maybe feeling guilty for thinking it.

Two

By Monday, everyone had a theory: Nancy had run off because she was pregnant; Nancy had been kidnapped by two strange men in a dark red car that ran a light at Madison and Beacon on Thanksgiving eve; Nancy had been murdered by Wallace Romola. Silver Henning had to bring Wallace in because of all the calls he received over the weekend, people swearing Wallace had been acting suspiciously on the town common the night Nancy disappeared. Nancy would have walked across the common on her way home.

"Poor Wallace," Mom said at breakfast Monday morning.

"He'll be free by noon," said Dad.

"But it's a shame for him to be put through that."

"Maybe he did it," Jerram said, lifting a spoonful of cereal to his mouth and missing. His eyes were on his history book, busily cramming for the exam he hadn't studied for all weekend.

Mom looked horrified. "How can you say such a thing? Wallace is a harmless boy."

"Wallace is thirty-six years old," Dad said.

"Wallace is brain dead," said Jerram.

"He is not," Rose butted in. "If people would just accept him the way he is, let him live his life his way, he'd be perfectly fine."

Her mother patted her arm. They agreed that Wallace was misunderstood. The Romolas were one of the richest families in town. They owned a winery and lived in a mansion on Swan Drive. When Wallace was sixteen, they gave him a Lamborghini sports car for his birthday. He totaled it the next day. He dropped out of high school and got a job pumping gas, and the Romolas realized he'd never be able to take over the family business. Now he hung out on the common, wearing rags and begging for money. People who didn't know he was a millionaire felt sorry for him and gave him small change. Rose had seen him laugh, slyly and secretly, when he thought no one was watching. Wallace was probably a lot smarter than he let on, but that didn't mean he'd murder anybody.

"Bus!" Mom announced. Jerram groaned and drank the rest of his cereal from the bowl. Rose grabbed her knapsack and parka, and they ran out the door just as the bus came rolling toward the driveway.

Her best friend Grace had saved her a seat. She wanted to talk about Nancy. They'd talked about it on the phone all weekend, but Grace was still bursting with theories. She rattled on until she realized Rose wasn't paying attention.

"Okay," she said, "so you think I'm being ghoulish."

"Maybe a little."

"But you're the most ghoulish person I know."

"I'm not."

"You are. You love it," Grace said with conviction.

"I don't. I detest horror movies."

"That's not what I mean. I mean all your stuff, you know, astral planes and psychic awareness."

"There's nothing ghoulish about that."

She made a face. "It's ghoulish to read people's minds. I, personally, for one, would not like someone reading my mind."

"You've got it all wrong," Jerram said from the seat behind. "A ghoul is a person who robs graves."

"So?" Grace challenged, turning around. "Isn't that just the right word? If you read a person's mind, it's like robbery."

"It'd have to be a dead mind to qualify," Jerram said. "But that's not hard." He gestured around the bus. "Take your pick."

Of course the whole school was talking about Nancy. At midmorning, there was a PA announcement that counselors would be available in the gym during lunch and after school if anyone wanted to talk things out.

"That means she's dead," Grace whispered. "They only have counselors when someone dies."

It began to bother Rose then, remembering the strange encounter last winter. Nancy had been in trouble, and she hadn't bothered to find out why. Could it have been related to this? She didn't want to go talk about it with the counselors, but she confessed to Grace.

"Don't do a guilt trip on yourself," Grace said. "You couldn't know then what would happen now. It was ages ago and probably some minor nothing."

"I know all that," Rose said, sounding ungrateful.

Grace never got ruffled by other people's bad tempers. "Well, maybe you should talk to a professional person. I'll go with you, if you like."

"The gym will be crawling with kids from her class. Let's not make fools of ourselves."

She had this nagging feeling, like someone softly breathing on the back of her neck. Once or twice she had to turn around, expecting to see someone there. In fact, once she thought she actually saw Nancy in the crowded hall: a glimpse of straggly blonde hair, a pink jacket. It gave her a funny feeling deep down inside. The kind of feeling you get when you think something bad is going to happen. It was crazy, but she was getting spooked. She wished they'd find Nancy, or at least find out what had happened.

At lunch, she phoned Mom to ask if there was news.

"No," Mom said. "But I'm sure I'll hear first thing from Barney." Barney — Mrs. Barnes — was their neighbor and the local Big Mouth. "Was Nancy a special friend? I didn't realize you knew her that well." Mom sounded worried.

"It's just that everybody's talking about it here."

"Don't let that imagination run away with you, Rose," Mom said.

"Nothing new," Rose told Grace when she hung up, and Grace said, "Well, no news is good news."

"Look, let's stop talking about it and thinking about it, okay?"

"Sure I'll stop talking, but I don't know if I can stop thinking," Grace said in her reasonable way.

"It has nothing to do with us. We weren't her friends. We didn't give her a single thought before; why are we upset now? We're just being sentimental."

Grace sighed. "You're probably right. People are always sorry after the fact." She looked at Rose earnestly. "But I'd be pretty upset if you disappeared."

"If I plan to vanish, I'll let you know."

Grace dragged her upstairs to the cafeteria. "Let's see if Gregory and Company are there."

"They're *always* there, Grace."

Grace was in love with Gregory Paschek. He acted as if she didn't exist, although he had been known to make eye contact on occasion. In fact, he sat on her beach towel twice last summer — without saying a word — and looked at her in the hall on September 11th and October 19th. Grace remembered these events, she took notes.

Gregory and Company did not seem to have been affected by Nancy's disappearance. They were sitting at their usual window table, throwing pasta shells at each other.

Grace mooned over, dragging Rose. Gregory

looked up for a moment and got a shot of pasta sauce in the eye for his trouble.

"Need a tissue, Gregory?" Grace asked. She said if she openly acted like a moo cow, she could pretend it was all a joke and make Gregory think she didn't take him seriously.

"Hi, Rose," Gregory said, ignoring Grace's tissue and wiping his face on his sleeve.

"Hi, Rose, Hi, Grace," said Paul and Randy.

"Hi, Grace, Hi, Rose," said Daniel.

"Hi, you all," Grace said, curling her fingers over into a silly wave.

"You're too late for lunch," Daniel said, looking straight at Rose in a disconcerting way. They cared about each other, Rose thought, but they kept dancing around instead of making real contact. Grace's outrageous behavior gave them cover; people were too busy watching Grace and Gregory act up to notice Rose and Daniel staring at each other. Sooner or later, Rose thought, something's got to give. But who was going to give in first?

"We had yogurt in art," Grace said, batting her eyes. "Valerian doesn't mind if we eat in class."

"They ate in art," said Paul, and this cracked the rest of them up. They fell around the table laughing and punching each other and not noticing that Daniel just sat there quietly looking at Rose. The noise of the cafeteria receded, and it was as if they were suddenly alone. A shiver of possibilities went through her, quickly squelched by that persistent underlying hesitation, worrying that Daniel would disappoint her by acting as jerky as the rest of them. Jerram said she had unreasonable expectations about men, which came from his being her twin brother and absolutely perfect. Jerram never hung out with guys in the cafeteria. But Jerram never did anything anybody else did.

There was dance class that afternoon so Rose took the town bus instead of going back with Grace. Daniel rode it, too, and it was accepted that they sat together. The conversation was not always a success. Rose was never sure of Daniel's mood. He could be friendly and open and they'd talk. Or he could be preoccupied and distant, making Rose feel shy and uncertain. Nervousness brought out the worst kind of Jerram-like remarks, witty but caustic, and she'd hate herself afterwards. Why was it always so hard to just act natural around Daniel?

"How's it going?" he said as she sat down. He smelled of tomato sauce.

"Okay . . . I guess."

"Yeah, I know what you mean. A heavy day. What do you think about it?"

"About Nancy? I'm not sure," Rose began but Daniel seemed eager to voice his own theories.

"She probably hitched a ride when she left the Berrys'. Faster to get to the mall than walking. It's the only way it could have happened, really, that she went along with it."

Rose felt shocked. "You mean, it's all her fault?"

Daniel looked surprised. "No, nothing like that. I just meant it was probably someone she knew. Somebody she trusted."

"But it makes it even more horrible."

"I've heard that most murders are committed by people the victims know." Daniel looked so pleased with his theory, Rose felt a twinge of distaste.

"Wonderful," she said sarcastically.

"Well, what do *you* think happened?"

"I really don't want to talk about it, if you don't mind," she snapped.

"Okay, fair enough," Daniel said, unperturbed, and looked at her as if waiting for the next move. But Rose couldn't think of anything to say after that. It was sickening. What did people talk about before Nancy disappeared? she wondered. When she got off the bus she heard Daniel say goodbye. Softly, softly, underneath the words there was still a promise. Wasn't there?

She was thankful for dance class. She could forget anything once she was out on the floor working. Only the movement and the music mattered, her muscles responding. She'd been studying with Muriel for five years, ever since Muriel came to town one snowy Christmas and opened up her school. It had been like a dream come true for Rose, a real teacher from New York instead of plump Mrs. Drury who taught ballet and tap in the basement of her home. Muriel had introduced Rose to modern dance: bare feet and freedom of movement instead of the constricting toe shoes and exacting positions of ballet. More than anything, Rose wanted to go on to study in New York. But was she good enough? Muriel said she was the best student she had, but Rose wasn't naive enough to think being the best dancer in Bethboro, Connecticut, meant the best in New York City.

Muriel wasn't just a teacher, she was a friend. They talked about things Rose couldn't discuss with her mother. Muriel listened differently and responded differently. Her advice never sounded like advice at all. If Rose had a problem, Muriel would say, "Sit in it like Buddha." Sit in it — experience it — live it — know it, and the answer would appear. Muriel had the kinds of ideas nobody else had. She seemed mysterious and glamorous, and Rose often wondered why she had come at all to a small town like Bethboro because although she was here, it was as if part of her was somewhere else at the same time.

Nobody mentioned Nancy Emerson in class; they talked about the Christmas recital in which Rose had a solo. She loved performing and got a rush onstage, feeling the audience reacting. But the Muriel Westa School of Dance recitals could be as corny as Mrs. Drury's, with the younger kids doing the "Waltz of the Flowers," clutching hoops of wax roses, and the tap students hoofing to "Broadway Melody," sounding like a herd of buffalo.

Rose walked home after class. Their house was on the ridge, not far from town. The evening had the sort of electric crackle that made her feel the world was full of possibilities and she could try them all. She allowed herself a small regret for the conversation with Daniel that afternoon, for being snappy and self-involved, as if Nancy's disappearance were some personal problem. A missed opportunity to have an intelligent discussion with him. She was good at missing opportunities like that.

I'm backward, she thought. Maybe from growing up so close to Jerram. Her crushes on boys had always been long-distance. She'd never had to participate in liking someone. With Jerram, it was as easy as liking herself, a thing hardly noticed. With Daniel, it was like having to learn the lines of a play. So far, she wasn't a very good actor. She'd tried to talk to Jerram about it once, thinking he could give her advice from the male side. But he hadn't been helpful. He seemed annoyed with her questions and annoyed with the idea of Daniel, so she gave up.

Her mother was standing in the driveway, looking down the hill.

"Rosecleer!" She called in her no-nonsense voice, but it sounded shaky. "Didn't you get my message?"

"What message?"

She turned away in exasperation, marched up to the house and held the door. When Rose was inside, she shut it firmly and turned the double lock. She looked hot and flustered.

"Muriel Westa needs her head examined! I specifically told her to make sure you got a ride with Mary Jo's mother."

"But I always walk."

"I don't want you walking after dark anymore."

"Oh, Mom!" Rose was going to say how silly it was, when she realized that five days ago Nancy would have said the same thing. Nancy would have laughed at her mother insisting she get a ride home. "Come on," she would have said, "what could possibly happen?" And yet, what if Daniel was right and it had been someone Nancy knew? Then a ride home wouldn't protect you at all.

"Sorry, Mom. But it's like living under siege. I'm getting sick of it. Nobody talks about anything but Nancy Emerson."

"I know. It's awful to think there's someone out there." She went to the window and cupped her hand over the glass so she could see into the dark. "People can't help being afraid of him."

Resisting a shiver, Rose asked, "Who's this *him*, anyway? We don't *know* what happened, Mom. It's going to be a really big laugh when Nancy comes waltzing back home."

"I'll be the first to laugh if that happens."

There was no escape. The Emersons were on the late news that night. Horrible interviews that made Rose wriggle with embarrassment. Mr. Emerson made a plea for Nancy's safe return. He had tears in his eyes, his voice broke, yet it seemed ludicrously like a TV miniseries instead of real life. The newscaster wore a silly half smile the whole time he talked about it, as if he'd forgotten how to erase his permanently pleasant TV face. "We're all praying for you, Nancy," he said. "And now this. . . ." An ad for snowblowers came on.

Mom told them to go to bed. She said it a few times politely, then got tough.

Jerram stuck his top teeth over his lower lip and gave an evil leer. "I nevair sleep at night. In the night, in the dark, I feed on the bloooood, and the blooood is the life."

Mom began to laugh, then clamped her mouth shut. "Jerram, please, don't talk about blood after that broadcast."

He had the decency to look abashed.

"Fear is like thick syrup," Jerram said as he and Rose went upstairs. "If you're not careful, it spills and you get covered with it."

"Is that advice? Because if it is, I'm not planning to spill any syrup on myself. I'm putting Nancy Emerson out of my mind."

"Good for you," Jerram said. "Eat your pancakes plain."

"Sometimes you're weird."

"That's always my intention."

"Good night," Rose said, but knew Jerram would stay up for hours yet, reading, studying, doing whatever things he did at night. He wasn't a vampire, but he did seem to feed on the night.

She washed her face and brushed her teeth. Got into bed and fell asleep almost instantly. And had a dream.

Three

IT HARDLY SEEMED LIKE A DREAM AT FIRST. SHE was asleep in her bed, in her room, and everything was the way it always was. But then, a lot of extra space suddenly appeared in between the furniture, so that things were dotted here and there on a vast expanse of floor. It looked like a painting by Salvador Dali, where everything seems stretched out.

Instead of the double sash window there were French doors leading onto a balcony. The moon was shining in a bright, uncanny way over the tips of pine trees and distant mountains.

Someone was standing on the balcony, looking in. It was unsettling to have someone staring in at her from the dark, but she recognized who it was: Nancy Emerson.

"What are you doing here?" Rose said, feeling more annoyed than scared. "Everyone's worried about you; you'd better go home."

Nancy just stood there and smiled. Then she shook her head, and a sparkling of tears scattered from her eyelashes. She put out her hand, and it reached across the room from the balcony to Rose's bed. "Could you come with me for a minute?" she said.

It felt warm and safe in bed, in spite of the stretched room and Nancy's weird arm. It looked strange outside, and Rose suddenly noticed there was something wrong with Nancy. She was transparent. And she looked ridiculous. She was wearing a huge red flower on her pink down jacket. Very bad taste.

"I don't want to." Rose's voice sounded like that of a whiny two-year-old.

"Please," Nancy said. She took a step into the room, the moonlight shining through her body. "I'm in trouble, and I don't know what to do."

Rose got up then, feeling very grouchy and making a big deal of finding her blue jeans and putting them on, and then there was one of those asides that occur in dreams, where you do nonsensical things. In this case, it was about whether to wear gray socks or red socks. All the gray socks had holes in the toes, and all the red socks were too long, stretching and stretching until they went up to her waist. She decided on red finally, to match the stupid flower Nancy was wearing.

Finally they stood out on the balcony, looking down at the tips of the pine trees. Nancy took Rose's hand and they lifted up, easy as pie, and flew off into the air.

Rose thought: I always knew I could do this. She tried some dance steps. Wouldn't Muriel be surprised!

They flew for a while and it got cold and then

boring. Finally they descended and landed in a forest. There were pine trees all around, and a prickly yet cushiony carpet of pine needles underfoot. Rose looked down and saw her red socks. She'd forgotten to wear shoes.

"So, what's the big deal?" she asked in her squeaky, two-year-old dream voice.

"There," Nancy said and pointed with her stretchy see-through arm at a small mound on the ground.

"I don't see nothing," Rose said and laughed. "Oops, bad grammar." She shook her finger at Nancy, and it became long and wobbly and fell over onto the back of her hand.

Nancy gave her a sad, forebearing smile. "I'm in trouble and I need help," she repeated. But Rose was noticing that the sun was coming up, with razor-sharp rays that cut her eyes. There was a sudden whiff of salt, a smell redolent of the sea and also of the brackish taste of blood. The red flower was leaking down Nancy's jacket. The sun blasted them like a bomb, and the dream disappeared.

It must be morning, Rose thought, but when she woke it was still dark. She lay there with pounding heart, trying to be sure she was really awake. The window and the furniture were normal again.

She got up and opened her bedroom door and peered out. The house was silent, but Jerram's light still came from under his door. She walked across the hall. Jerram was at the door almost before she lifted a hand. They had always had a kind of mental communication between them, knowing what the other needed or wanted. But lately the bond between them seemed to be growing weaker.

"What's up?" Jerram asked.

"I had a dream . . . about Nancy Emerson."

Jerram drew her in and shut the door. His room was a litter of projects, not enough desktops or tables to accommodate them all, so some were set out on the floor. It only looked like a mess to an untrained eye. It was laid out with orderly precision.

"What about it?" Jerram asked.

"It was more than a dream. It was as vivid as if it had been really happening, as if Nancy had come here tonight to tell me something. Why me, Jerram? I'm not her friend."

"I don't know. Just tell me the dream."

"We flew over a pine forest. It was nice. It was as if I always knew I could fly. Why are you smiling like that?"

"Everyone knows flying in dreams is sexual."

"Come on, Jerram, I was hardly having a sexual dream. She was wearing a red flower. So red. Blood-red. Do you think it was blood? Do you think Nancy was trying to tell me she's been hurt?"

"You need to go back." Jerram was serious now. "Get in touch with exactly what you did and saw. Redream it, but stay awake when you do."

She closed her eyes. The balcony, the silly search for gray or red socks, the forest, the mound of pine needles, the flower running red.

"I think she's dead, Jerram. And I think she was showing me where she was buried."

He put his arm around her, and she realized she was shaking. "It's okay, it's okay. Take it easy. Breathe."

He breathed with her, getting her calm. They sat together on his bed, his arm around her, hugging her the way he used to do when they were kids and Mom or Dad had yelled about some mischief. She felt safe with Jerram's arm around her, his body close. He has always been like a half of me, she thought, and lately the half has been missing a lot.

The sky began to lighten. She went back to her own room. "Thanks," she said, groggy with sleep.

Jerram wasn't the least bit sleepy. "Tomorrow," he said, "you'll have to tell someone about this dream."

Four

THE BETHBORO POLICE STATION WAS A BRAND-new chunk of beige cement surrounded by a parking lot. Inside, were plastic plants and the smell of Lysol; it looked nothing like *Hill Street Blues* reruns. Rose and Grace gawked hesitantly before they went up to the young policeman presiding at the big sweep of front desk. Rose asked to speak to Silver Henning.

"What for?"

Explaining a dream to a cop wasn't going to be easy. "It's confidential," she said.

The policeman sat up straighter and pursed his lips. "Who are you?"

"Rosecleer Potter."

"Rose who?"

"Rose Potter," Grace piped up. "It's very important for her to see Chief Henning."

"He's busy. You'd better tell me whatever you want to tell him."

Rose dithered, not wanting to explain a dream in full view of the door and the plastic plants.

Grace said reasonably, "Could we see a detective instead?"

The policeman gave a condescending smile. "You can't see anybody until you tell me what it's all about."

Rose was ready to argue the point, but Grace blurted, "Nancy Emerson."

"Why didn't you say so?" He picked up a phone, pushed some buttons, mumbled into it and told them to go upstairs and turn right at the coffee machine. "Detective O'Hara," he said.

"Detective O'Hara," Grace whispered as they climbed the antiseptic staircase. "A big beefy guy with a red nose and a chip on his shoulder. Chain-smoker, too. Our hair will stink. My mother will accuse me of smoking again. I'll have to take a shower at your house before I go home."

"Stop chattering," Rose said. "I'm nervous, too."

"Who's nervous? I was theorizing."

They made a right at the coffee machine and found the room. The door was ajar but they hesitated, debating whether to walk right in or knock.

"Come on in, girls," a pleasantly sweet voice called out.

Detective O'Hara wasn't big or beefy. She was slim, blonde and young-looking, sitting behind a desk littered with diet Pepsi cans. She was chewing one of her long red fingernails. She inspected the nail critically before waving them into the hard metal chairs in front of her desk. Her gold bracelets clinked.

"What can I do for you, girls?" she asked chummily.

It was a little disappointing. Rose had expected eager anticipation to hear anything about the Emerson case. Instead the detective sat there, relaxed and smiling, as if she could care less. Rose felt tongue-tied.

Grace cleared her throat, a signal that Rose should get on with it.

"This is going to sound weird. I really don't know how to start."

"Start at the beginning," Detective O'Hara said. "It's always the best place."

"Well, it's not really a beginning. Unless you count last night. I — "

"She had a dream," Grace forged ahead. "About Nancy Emerson."

Detective O'Hara didn't laugh. She nodded, her face calm, and she sneaked another look at her nails. Rose plunged in.

"All right, I had a dream. But it wasn't the usual kind of dream. It was very real, as if it were happening. As if it were . . . some kind of message."

It was gratifying to see Detective O'Hara pick up a notebook and pencil. "Just tell me the content."

"Nancy took me with her to some kind of woods. I think she'd been hurt. She had blood, here." Rose touched her chest at the spot where Nancy had worn the red flower. "I think she's in that woods. I think . . . she's dead."

"Which woods?"

"I don't know."

O'Hara looked up, eyes a little suspicious now. "Nearby?"

"I don't know at all. Except there were pine trees and lots of pine needles."

"Any other landmarks?"

She thought back to flying with Nancy. She hadn't been paying enough attention. "No. Sorry."

Detective O'Hara put down the pencil and folded her hands in front of her, the red nails like little dots of blood on her arms.

"I know this has been upsetting for all you kids. But we're working on this twenty-four hours a day. What you can do to help is . . ." She put up her hand and ticked off the points on her long fingers: "One, stay cool, stay calm, don't go off the deep end. You're perfectly safe in Bethboro, and we have extra patrols out at night. Two, once you're calm, think back. Did you see or hear anything that night? Only facts can help us. Even something you don't think is important. Three, if you're upset, get help. Speak to your parents, speak to your school counselor. Don't bottle it up inside." She smiled benignly.

Rose realized they had been dismissed. Obviously O'Hara thought Rose was bottling things up and ready to pop a cork. The way words were emphasized — "only facts" — told them what O'Hara thought about a dream.

"Come on, Grace." Rose got up and headed for the door. But Grace kept sitting.

"I thought the police used information from people who have psychic powers," she said, her cheeks growing red. "I've seen it on television; it's taken seriously. Rose isn't doing this for a joke. She's not like that."

Detective O'Hara leaned back and sighed.

"I appreciate your coming in," she said in that kind of soft voice people use when they think you're nuts but don't want to hurt your feelings. She looked up at Rose. "Tell me, have you done this kind of thing before? Received psychic messages?"

"No," Rose said. "No psychic messages." Grace opened her mouth in protest, wanting to tell all about how Rose and Jerram used to say they could read each other's minds, but Rose gave her a hard, warning look.

"Let's go, Grace," she urged, and Grace reluctantly heaved herself out of the uncomfortable chair.

"Thanks, girls. Come back to see me if you remember anything about the night Nancy disappeared."

"I suppose you believe poor Wallace Romola did it," Grace said over her shoulder as a feeble parting shot.

Detective O'Hara didn't answer. Outside in the hall, Grace blew out her cheeks and fanned herself. "What a bitch."

"It was a silly idea to come here."

"You should have let me tell her about you and Jerram."

"It would only have made things worse. Besides, that's sort of typical with twins. We're tuned into each other, or at least we were. It's not the same as getting a message from the dead."

Grace shivered. "Oooh, don't put it that way."

"But that's what it is, isn't it, if Nancy is really buried in a pine woods somewhere?"

"I guess."

"Let's just forget it."

"But shouldn't we do something?"

"What can we do?"

Grace thought a moment and shrugged helplessly, her face pinched.

"Listen, Nancy's alive — just wait and see," she said, trying to convince herself as much as comfort Rose. "They have posters as far away as New York. I heard somebody called from there and said they saw her at the Port Authority bus station — that's a place where all the runaways hang out. Maybe Nancy was a secret druggie."

Rose squeezed her hand. "It's all right, Grace. Let's forget it."

"You said that before. But neither one of us is forgetting it."

Grace shoved her hands down inside the pockets of her yellow jacket and marched along. Rose promised herself she wasn't spending another minute thinking about Nancy Emerson. She wasn't hysterical with fear as O'Hara implied, didn't imagine danger was lurking all over Bethboro. The town looked the same. And nobody else had disappeared.

Since the detective hadn't been the chain-smoker Grace feared, she could go home without washing her long black hair. Rose trudged along to her own house, refusing the temptation to find the spot where she'd encountered Nancy last year. Jerram wanted to know all about the visit to the police.

She told him what had happened. "So that's it. There's nothing more I can do."

"There is one thing . . ." Jerram said.

"No, thanks, I've got a history paper due."

She could feel Jerram's mind pulling at her. When he was determined, his mind became an octopus, sending out tentacles. He could force her to listen to him when he wanted to. Of course, it used to be stronger, and it used to be worse because when they were little, Jerram always wanted help with his pranks. Some of them were fairly innocent, like sneaking cookies before dinner. Others were gross, like Jerram smearing himself with ketchup and making Rose run screaming to Mom that he'd hurt himself. Now he looked at her with those pale blue eyes that were so like her own. She sighed. "Okay, what is it?"

"You could go see Old Mackey. He's got the Celtic personality for things like dream messages. He'll believe you."

"O'Hara sounds pretty Celtic, too, and she didn't."

"Too modern, dependent on technology," Jerram sneered in spite of the technology littering his room. "You tell Mackey and he'll make them listen, being he was police chief for so many years."

"They'll just think he's as silly as I am."

"He's an institution in this town."

"But I don't know him or even where he lives."

"He's up on North Hill. Pronounce his name Mac - eye if you want him to talk to you." Jerram paused and looked sheepish. "He has a nasty temper."

"Thanks a bunch."

"Don't worry, though. He's an old sweetheart if you get on his good side."

"And how do I do that?"

"Cookies. He likes peanut butter cookies. They're his favorite. Bake him some, he won't eat store-bought."

She looked at Jerram. "And how do you know all this?"

"Tried a toilet paper mushball on him the Halloween you were in bed with your toes. He hit me back with a snowball. Had a pile of them in his freezer from the winter before. We called it a draw, and he invited me in."

It came back. "*That* was why you came home with no treats for me. I never believed that story you told about giving the candy away to the poor starving children you'd met."

He chuckled, remembering. "Mom's still convinced I ate it all myself."

"Jerram, I'm afraid of getting into this."

Jerram considered. "Well, there's one hope. Mackey won't believe you, either, and then you *can* forget it."

"I'll think about it."

She went to get started on the paper. It was on the Salem witch trials in terms of modern psychology, and it had to be good. Mr. Keller, the history teacher, hadn't been enthusiastic about the choice. "I trust you not to give us a horror film version," he'd said. He didn't have to worry. Most of the victims accused of witchcraft in 1692 had never even given it a thought. It was people attacking what they didn't understand. Maybe attacking what they were afraid was inside themselves.

Involved with the writing, she really did forget about Nancy and the dream. It wasn't until turning out the light to go to sleep that it came back. She looked nervously toward the window, dreading to see Nancy staring in. It would have been nice to have her old night-light. For a while, after Jerram and she got their own rooms, she'd had a bad case of the night creeps — thinking monsters were under the bed, the usual stuff. It would be easy to get them back again.

No way, she decided. No way would she go up North Hill to tell Old Mackey about dreams, Celtic as he might be. Forget it. She was going to mind her own business.

Five

THE HISTORY CLASS BEGAN GIVING THE PAPERS aloud on Monday, thirteen days after Nancy's disappearance. Mr. Keller asked Rose to be first.

"Rosecleer will enlighten us on the subject of witches," he announced in his most pompous voice.

Gregory made a hooing noise in the back of the room.

"You have something to say, Mr. Paschek?"

"Who? Me? No. Well. It's like scary, you know?"

The rest of the class joined in.

"Seriousness, please!" Mr. Keller raised his voice.

"The year 1697 was a year of guilt," Rose began. "The village of Salem, Massachusetts, realized they'd made a mistake. People who had taken part in the collective hysteria admitted they'd been wrong. Of course, they blamed the Devil . . ." More noises began in the back row, echoes of "the Devil made me do it." Mr. Keller rapped his ruler on the desk. Rose took a breath and went on.

"But the people of Salem needed an excuse. It wasn't easy to face up to the fact that twenty innocent people had been executed and more than 100 imprisoned, some of them expectant mothers who were forced to have their babies in jail." Sniggers erupted.

"But these were small numbers compared with the thousands of victims of witch hunts in Europe. Salem can be looked upon as a microcosm — "

Mr. Keller interrupted her. "Are you quoting all this, Rosecleer?"

"Quoting?"

"Reading what you've copied from a book."

"No, of course not, Mr. Keller."

He made a dismissive gesture. "Continue."

She told how the witch trials began, with a group of young girls bored out of their skulls in the puritanical New England winter. The Company wouldn't stop cracking jokes. Rose knew Mr. Keller was going to tell her to sit down in a minute. If you couldn't present your paper convincingly to the class, you failed. Then Daniel shouted, "Hey, you guys, shut up. I want to hear this."

Mr. Keller made a fishy face, but said nothing. Suddenly everybody shut up and listened. And they liked it. When she told about the lawsuits some of the accused brought on their accusers, they got really into it.

"Seven pounds, six shillings? How much is that, Mr. K? They should have sued for a million dollars."

"Well done, Rosecleer," Mr. Keller said. She

sat down, sweaty and pleased, remembering it was Daniel who got everybody to shut up. Daniel, making a public statement about her. She didn't dare look back to catch his eye.

"We have just enough time for one more," Mr. Keller said. "I call on Gregory Paschek."

Serves him right for heckling me, Rose thought. Gregory shuffled up to the front of the room, his face red as a beet. His paper was on the Plimouth Plantation, totally predictable and safe, except for a brilliant flourish at the end when he made a comparison with Roman estates. Mr. Keller, who had been gazing out the window and probably thinking about his shopping list for the Stop and Save after work, suddenly sat up and blinked. Before he had a chance to challenge Gregory's unusually deep thought, the bell rang.

Grace was in the hall.

"You looked wiped out," she said.

"I gave my paper. Mr. K. made me go first."

Grace's eyes searched over Rose's shoulder, looking for her one and only.

"Gregory didn't help much," Rose told her. "I don't know what you see in that idiot."

"Did he give his paper?" she asked, oblivious to the complaints.

"Yes, he was second."

"Did he do okay? I hope he used the stuff I told him."

"Like about the Roman estates?"

"Yeah, did he?"

"It was a smashing success. Keller almost dropped his teeth."

Grace looked pleased. "I got it from this book my father has."

"You shouldn't have. Keller will never believe Gregory could think up a thing like that."

Grace's face clouded. "I hope he doesn't get into trouble. Where is he? Maybe I should ask him. . . ."

"Come on, Grace. Art. Gregory can take care of himself."

At lunchtime, Gregory and Company were in the cafeteria, at their regular table. Grace wanted to sit as near to them as possible but by the time they got through the line, there was no room and no chance to see Daniel, either.

After school was dance class, but he wasn't on the bus because of basketball practice. Rose felt a flutter in her stomach that was growing familiar. When Daniel wasn't there, it seemed so urgent to see him. Then, when he was, she clammed up.

She stayed late after class to rehearse her solo with Muriel. They had choreographed it together, but it was loose enough for Rose to change things as she went along, to fit her mood.

Muriel's studio was a long, high-ceilinged room above Robando's Real Estate and Beckley's Insurance, in an old-fashioned building facing the town common. It had once been an apartment, but Muriel had taken out all the walls and redecorated it with professional efficiency, making it look like a real studio, with an office and dressing room at the back. She left the four floor-to-ceiling windows in the big main practice room, and when it got dark you could see the lights winking through the trees. Rose was moving across the floor toward the windows in a series of traveling jumps when it happened. The music urged her forward, soaring from Muriel's big speakers at the other end of the room. Vivaldi's Violin Concerto in C minor, *Il Sospetto* — it whirled and climbed, broke like a heartbreak, then climbed in joy again. And as Rose danced toward the lights of the common, the windows suddenly vanished. She felt herself rise off the floor, not just a jump but flying through the air as she'd done with Nancy, in a great rush of wind, music and dark. Up and up, with Nancy's voice calling out. It was cold. Icy. Ice crystals formed on her bare arms, threatening to drag her down from the height. She tried to keep moving, though, because Nancy had begun to scream.

"Rose! Rose! For God's sake, stop!"

Not Nancy. Muriel screaming.

She banged hard up against the ice-cold window. Her face stared back wide-eyed, reflected against the flickering dark. Muriel rushed across the room. "Are you all right? Are you hurt? My God, you could have gone right through the glass." She took off her big paisley shawl and wrapped it around Rose, hugged her safe with her hard, muscular arms. Slowly, Rose became aware of Muriel's familiar, expensive perfume and the faint odor of sweat.

"What on earth happened to you?"

"Flying," Rose said. "It was like flying."

"Rose! Look at me. Are you all right?"

She was stunned but she was coming back. "Yes. Fine now."

"You frightened me."

"Shouldn't have skipped lunch. I got dizzy," she lied.

"I thought as much." Muriel held her at arm's length, searching Rose's blue eyes. Muriel's own eyes were deep and brown, with crinkled edges that made her look as if she'd seen a lot of sadness and pain.

"You work too hard, Rose. I'm against nagging, but I have to say this. Go easy on yourself. This solo isn't that important. If it's meant for you to be a dancer, you will. You're a good dancer, but it's tough out there and — "

"I know. I know what you mean."

She nodded. "I wish I could help you more. I want you to make it, if that's what *you* want. I want you to have it all, not be like me. . . ." She gestured to the room. "A small-time dance teacher in a one-horse town."

Behind her eyes, there seemed to be things she could not say. How often Rose had thought Muriel had come to Bethboro for some other reason than opening a school. Muriel liked to joke that she enjoyed being a big fish in a small pond, not like New York where she was a little sardine. But Rose had seen her when she thought she wasn't being observed, sitting alone in her half-shadowed office, gazing into space, brooding.

Now she shivered and rubbed her hands briskly over her leotard-clad arms. "Come on, get dressed. I'm going to drive you home."

"It's okay, I can walk."

"Not on those jellyfish legs."

Muriel put a sweater and slacks over her leotards and threw on the big black cloak she always wore for effect. She switched off the lights and closed and locked the door. The telephone began to ring as they went down the stairs. Muriel stopped and looked undecided. "I'm fine," Rose said. "Go back and answer it." Muriel gave herself a shake and smiled. "Maybe it's fated for me to miss this one," she said. Muriel was always talking about fate.

They clumped down the stairs and outside to Muriel's car. The air was cold, with the fresh tang of good things to come. Christmas air. Rose took a deep breath. The trees on the common sparkled with tiny golden Christmas lights. A man came toward them, hunched against the cold, wearing a ripped overcoat that had once been expensive, with a large woman's scarf tied over the shoulders. A dirty-looking wool hat was jammed on his head. His hands, held forward as if begging, were bare.

"Who's that?" Muriel said in a frightened voice, backing away.

"It's only Wallace Romola. He must be freezing."

Muriel let out a breath that frosted in the air. "Oh, him. Well, it's his choice, isn't it? It's not as if he doesn't have a home to go to."

"I don't think he gets along with his family."

Muriel was unsympathetic. "You can't feel

sorry for him, though, can you? He gives me the creeps."

"He's harmless." Rose defended Wallace as she always did.

"That may be, but I don't like it. He's hanging around too much lately."

"He always hangs around the common. He's sort of the town mascot."

Muriel unlocked her car and hustled Rose in. Wallace had stopped a few yards away and was staring intently. Ignoring him, Muriel got in quickly, slammed the door and turned the key in the ignition. "I don't know what he wants from me."

"He asks everybody for money."

She shrugged. "He always looks so stricken. The other day he came right up to me. His mouth was going a mile a minute but nothing came out. It was disgusting."

It was obvious that Muriel didn't like Wallace, so Rose didn't try to explain how Wallace had a hard time making himself understood, how he couldn't always talk properly to people. They drove on making small talk until reaching Rose's house. Muriel touched her arm. "I shouldn't say this. But maybe you need it tonight." She laughed a little nervously. "Or maybe it's just what you don't need. Anyway, I'm going to ask a . . . friend to come up for the recital. Someone who knows dance. He might be able to help you."

"From New York?"

She put a finger to her lips. "Mum's the word for now."

Rose felt energized. A dance person from New York . . . which company? Was it a chance? A scholarship? She jumped out of the car.

" 'Bye, Rose. And calm down! Too much excitement can give you leg cramps."

A bright oblong of light broke the darkness on the front path as Mom opened the door. "Rosecleer. I'm glad you got a ride home. I was waiting for your call."

Rose had forgotten all about it.

"Sorry. Muriel drove me; nothing to worry about."

Mom shut the front door, looking grim.

"Lots to worry about," she said. "The police have been to see Grace. What did you girls say at the police station last week? What did you think you were doing?"

"We didn't do anything. . . ."

"They'll probably be here next. They think you and Grace know something about Nancy's murder. They asked her all kinds of questions about Wallace Romola. Rose, did you see Wallace and Nancy that night?"

"No, Wallace has nothing to do with it!" She stopped. "Mom, what did you say?"

"You heard me. You implicated Wallace Romola."

"Not that, before that. Nancy's *murder*?"

Her mother sat down on the old church pew they kept in the hall. She had to push all the books and scarves and gloves aside to make space. She leaned over and put her elbows on her knees and cupped her chin in her hands. She looked up at Rose with despairing eyes.

"They found her body. She'd been stabbed to death."

Rose's heart thudded. She heard her voice coming out through layers and layers of wool. "Where?"

"It doesn't matter where. They found her, that's all."

"Where, Mom?"

She sighed distractedly. "Miles and miles from here, thank God. It must have been on the highway, somebody picked her up. Nobody from around here. Poor Wallace, of course he didn't do anything. He has no car. I hope Grace told them he has no car."

"They know that, Mom. *Where?*" Rose shouted.

"What's so important about where?" her mother retorted angrily.

Dad appeared in the living room doorway, wearing his halfmoon reading glasses, the evening newspaper in his hand. "Hey, hey, what's going on?"

"A lot of morbid nonsense," Mom grumbled and took herself off to the kitchen in a huffy way.

"She's worried," Dad said. "And rightly so, darlin'."

"Where was Nancy Emerson's body found, Dad?"

He peered at her over his reading glasses. "Somewhere near the Cape, in Massachusetts. She was buried in the woods."

Pine woods, scrub pine, pine needles. Rose was remembering one summer's rented house, gray clapboard salted by the sea breeze. Kicking up the thick carpet of brown pine needles with bare feet. It hurt a little.

She tasted the salty breeze in her mouth and wondered at it.

"Rose, Rose," her father was saying, putting his arms around her. "Stop crying, it's all right."

He thought she was weeping for Nancy. If only it was as simple as that.

Part Two

Him

SHE WHO IS MY SISTER NEVER UNDERSTOOD ME; she always blamed me, believing only what she wanted to believe. She's here, wicked and all-knowing person. Her voice, like gravebones, makes the taste of pain in my ear.

She never knew the truly me. Inside, where my blood boils, is where I really am, and I am ready to come alive again. Everything has its season and mine is now, as it always has been, the season of joy. I will again do what I must do. I am not afraid to do it.

Killing is not a bad thing. Death is easeful, death is kind. I am friends with death. It cools the boiling blood. Blood is as red as a Christmas ribbon. Blood ties a body like a Christmas package. Blood is the color of Christmas berries, baubles, all things of joy. Why shouldn't I find joy in blood?

This is a nice town. It has been a good place to hide, and it has been a good place to make death.

What is really amusing is that, in all these years, she has never known how close I am.

Rose

Six

SHE WENT TO JERRAM FOR COMFORT.

"We all get premonitions or have weird dreams once in a while," he said reasonably.

"Mine wasn't just a weird dream. It came true."

"For some reason there was a strong connection between you and Nancy. But it probably won't happen again."

"How can I be sure? I don't like the idea of having a direct line to the dead, Jerram. Or maybe I'm just going crazy, you know, hearing voices, having visions. Isn't that called schizophrenia?"

"You're not crazy."

"Maybe I need to see a psychiatrist."

"You don't need a psychiatrist. Come on."

"But I need to talk to someone, or I will go crazy."

"You're talking to me, aren't you?" Jerram frowned. "Although I wonder why, since you're not interested in my advice."

"What do you mean?"

"You never spoke to Old Mackey."

It was true, she hadn't.

"And of course you feel free to spout off to people, when it suits you," Jerram said in a tight voice.

"What people? I've only told you and that Detective O'Hara."

"And your friend."

"You mean Grace?"

Jerram gave the slightest sneer. "No, not Grace," he said impatiently. "I was thinking of that dingdong from the cafeteria."

Rose was befuddled. "Who?"

"What's-his-face. Daniel?"

She felt furious. "He is not a dingdong, if you don't mind. And I haven't told him anything." Jerram had been so solicitous a moment ago. Now he was agitated. He jumped up from the end of his bed and began to rearrange his untidy desk with his back to her. After a moment, he turned around and seemed more like her old Jerram again.

"I just want to protect you. People can be so cruel. You and me, we can accept sharing dreams, ESP. Outsiders will misunderstand."

"You're right, I know," she said, although she couldn't imagine Daniel being cruel in that way. "But look, why is it only me having these dreams? Why not you, too? We always dreamed the same dreams. How come you didn't dream about Nancy?"

Jerram's face was bleak. "I don't know."

They always used to share their dreams, especially when they had shared a room. Rose would dream the beginning and he'd dream the end. They told their parents about it and were punished for making up stories. Jerram, always the practical thinker, even at age ten, decided they'd better keep it quiet from then on. "It'll be our secret, Rose-ear," he'd said. He began writing the dreams down and still had the notebook somewhere. They thought they were safe, but they probably whispered about it too much, putting their heads together as soon as they woke up. Mom and Dad noticed. Visits to a psychologist ensued, tests and games with dolls and an invitation to share all kinds of private thoughts with the strange man with the black glasses.

They hated it. Rose was a little afraid, but Jerram suffered the most. One day, he just couldn't stand it anymore, and he called the psychologist a big ass to his face, grabbed Rose and pulled her out of the playroom before the session time had ended. He and Rose had waited on the corner for their parents, holding hands. Dad spoke to the psychologist and threatened Jerram with a spanking. But Mom said maybe Jerram should be given a chance to tell his side. Jerram made a speech, sitting at the kitchen table, pushing chocolate chip cookies into his mouth and gulping milk.

"He's scared of us," Jerram explained, with a big milk mustache around his mouth. "He pretends he's not, but he really is. He's afraid Rose-ear and me are gonna read his mind." Jerram laughed and sprayed milk and cookie crumbs all around.

Mom and Dad had looked at each other in astonishment. Dad cancelled the rest of the appointments and brought home an armload of books on twins. Perhaps their parents had been a little frightened, too. Perhaps the books had helped. But was it all over now? Had they stopped dreaming the same dreams? Jerram was angry in a way Rose didn't understand. Was he hiding something from her?

The police didn't believe in dreams. They wanted hard, cold facts. Silver Henning himself came to the house. He brought Detective O'Hara.

"Thought it would be more convenient if we came up here instead of asking the young lady to come to the station," the chief said to Mom. "More discreet, too."

"I hardly think it's discreet to have that car of yours parked out in my driveway," Mom said.

"Sorry, ma'am."

They wanted to know what Rose knew, not satisfied with what she'd told Detective O'Hara.

"Did you actually see Wallace Romola with Nancy that night?" the chief asked.

"He has nothing to do with all this."

"Ah, but you did mention him, didn't you? Now why would you do that?"

"I didn't mention him; Grace did. It was just a sarcastic remark because she was upset."

"Upset about what you two knew?"

"Upset with Detective O'Hara."

The chief raised his eyebrows and looked at O'Hara. She was wearing a suit and silk blouse and gold jewelry — a gold chain, and a gold pin on the lapel. Next to Chief Henning in his scruffy pants and worn leather jacket, she looked cool and elegant.

"I don't recall saying anything to upset you," she said to Rose.

"It was what you implied. Or what Grace thought you implied. It bothered her."

"Just what bothered your friend Grace?" the chief asked.

"I just told you. Detective O'Hara didn't believe me, and Grace got a little angry."

"And what exactly was it you told the detective?"

Rose looked at her mother, but Mom just shook her head helplessly. She knew about the dream. Rose had had to explain why she and Grace went to the police.

"Do I have to tell it all over again?" Rose asked.

"I'd like to hear it firsthand," the chief said, encouragingly. Mom interrupted to offer everybody coffee, and there was a pause while she got the cups and saucers and the coffeepot. Then Chief Henning listened attentively and Detective O'Hara took notes, a lot more than she'd taken the first time.

When Rose was done, the chief shook his head. "I can't help thinking you know something more. Something important." Mom began to protest, and he put up his hand in a mild warning. "Something she doesn't know she knows, Mrs. Potter," he said. "Something she saw without really seeing. It slipped into her subconscious and came out in the dream."

"That sounds reasonable," Detective O'Hara put in, smiling at Rose.

She didn't smile back. The slightest hint of hostility passed between them. Chief Henning began to expound again, but Mom interrupted him.

"Sweet potatoes," she said. "The only thing my daughter saw that night was sweet potatoes. She was in this house, in the kitchen, helping me get ready for Thanksgiving dinner."

Chief Henning shifted and carefully put his empty coffee cup down on the table. "Well, now, she might have slipped out . . ."

"Sweet potatoes, chopped celery, onions, chestnuts, bread crumbs," Mom raised a finger for each item. "You'd better write this down, Detective O'Hara. Where was I? Oh, yes, it was hard to peel the skins off some of the chestnuts. Then we did the giblets, boiled them up and diced the liver and gizzard for the gravy. It took us all evening. My husband and son will confirm it, lazy louts that they are."

"Now, Mrs. Potter," the chief began blustering.

"Silver, you've known me a long time."

He nodded.

"My daughter had a dream and that's all. She doesn't know anything else. Please be kind enough to leave her alone."

"Now, Liz," Chief Henning said.

"I mean it."

Detective O'Hara looked as if she wanted to make an arrest on the spot, but Silver Henning got up and started saying good-bye. Liz Potter interrupted him. "What's happened to poor Wallace, may I ask?"

"Free as a bird," the chief replied. "A friend of his gave him an alibi."

"Did he need an alibi, Silver?" she asked sharply.

The chief shrugged. "Not my place to say right now, Liz. But Wallace's friend is the soul of truth. Anyway, body was up at the Cape. I'll say, off the record mind you, that Wallace doesn't have it in him to travel that far."

Mom saw them to the door, asking questions that Chief Henning was reluctant to answer.

When she came back to the living room to clear up the cups and saucers she looked pensive. "Wallace's friend," she muttered. "I never heard of him having a friend."

"That doesn't mean he couldn't have one."

"Hmm." Mom sat down on the sofa holding an empty cup in her hands. "It must be that sister of his bailing him out of trouble again. She won't have him in the house yet she comes to his rescue."

"Wallace knows a lot of people. He may look like a bag person, but he's not stupid."

"Yes, I know you've always had a soft spot for Wallace. And I've been sympathetic, too. But maybe you shouldn't be too friendly for the time being."

Rose was horrified. "Mom, you're as bad as Silver Henning. I thought you agreed with me. Wallace didn't have anything to do with Nancy's murder and you know it."

"Well, we can't really know. . . ."

"You're acting just like they did in Salem," Rose cried, feeling suddenly drained and vulnerable. "You're picking on an innocent person out of fear."

"Rosecleer, mind your mouth," Mom said severely. She got up and took the cups into the kitchen.

Rose followed, bringing the coffeepot. "I'm sorry, it's just that I hate to see people accusing someone like Wallace only because he's different."

"I know, dear. It's admirable of you."

"Thanks, Mom . . ." Rose started to give her a hug and was surprised when her mother wriggled out of reach.

"Do me a favor, Rosecleer," she said, turning on the hot-water tap. "Don't have any more dreams!"

Seven

NANCY'S FUNERAL WAS PRIVATE. AFTER IT WAS over, the atmosphere in Bethboro lifted, as if everything was going to be all right now. There were only eighteen shopping days until Christmas. Christmas was a way for everybody to forget about murder.

Grace and Rose made plans to shop at the mall. Bethboro was a small town, and the mall was part of it. Walk out on Beacon Street, cross the highway, and you were there. The neighborhood was a little crummy for a couple of blocks, known as the town's tough section, where people hung out on dim front porches and sometimes shouted at you passing by. But now such incidents seemed silly to worry about.

Silver Henning's police force was still visible. There was a lot of pressure on him to solve the murder, but Silver was positive it was a crime of opportunity — that somebody just passing through had somehow got Nancy into his car and driven off with her. He called a conference to tell Bethboro they had no need to worry.

"We're talking about a stranger," he said. "This is not a homegrown crime."

Rose remembered what Daniel had said about getting murdered by someone you knew. But if the police chief was convinced otherwise, why worry? She wished she could talk to Daniel about it. She wished they could just be alone together, away from school and Gregory and Company. Wallace Romola had been cleared. He had an airtight alibi for the night Nancy disappeared. He hadn't wanted to tell about it because it was so private. But after he spent the night in jail, Martha Mackey, the former police chief's sister, came to get him out. She said that on the night of Nancy's disappearance, Wallace had been at her house, having a little supper and staying overnight, as he often did. There was no questioning her integrity. Besides, Miss Mackey had been Wallace's schoolteacher and was twenty years older than him.

"So, that's the friend!" Mom exclaimed. "Martha Mackey always did have a soft spot for strays."

"If it's true, why didn't he say so in the first place instead of keeping it a big secret?" Dad said.

"You mean, you think she's lying?" Rose asked.

"Well, no, I guess not," he said. "Anyway, nobody believed Wallace was guilty, so what difference does it make?"

"I never would have thought Miss Mackey would take in the likes of him," Mom said. "She keeps such a clean house."

Mom didn't really want Rose to walk to the mall, but she knew better than to forbid it. She made Rose agree to call so they could be picked up when they were ready to come home.

Grace wanted to buy Gregory Paschek a plaid wool shirt.

"What for?" Rose asked.

"For Christmas, what else?"

"I mean, why give him a present? He hardly talks to you."

"It's better to give than to receive," Grace said primly.

"Come on, that's not the reason."

Grace's cheeks flushed. "You know the reason perfectly well, Rose. Stop hassling me."

Rose trailed along after her into the men's shop. "It's just that I think it's wrong," she tried to explain. "You throwing yourself at him. I know you say you do it for a joke, but underneath it isn't a joke at all, is it?"

Grace refused to answer. She got busy looking at the plaid shirts.

"I mean, I think it's nice to be honest, show your feelings and all, but don't you think this is going too far?" Rose looked at the price tags. "Like forty-nine dollars too far? An expensive gift will embarrass him."

Grace stopped fingering the shirts. "Do you really think so?"

"Of course. He'll be mortified to get a gift like this. Not only expensive but personal."

Grace looked doubtful. "It's only a shirt, not a pair of underpants."

"But it goes next to his body. It's a sort of, I don't know, a motherly sort of gift."

Grace backed away from the display like it was

poison. "I never thought of it that way. Let's get out of here."

"I knew you'd see reason."

"The truth is I only have a hundred dollars to spend."

"Yeah . . . Gregory's not worth fifty percent."

"I'll get him something stupid instead."

"To match his personality."

Rose bought Jerram a new Swiss Army knife; he'd lost his, and he said he couldn't live without his portable scissors, toothpick, tweezers, etcetera. Jerram liked to leave the house in what he called a Totally Intact State, meaning he could survive in case there was a nuclear war or other catastrophe. This required a knife, Mini Mag flashlight, water purification tablets, a rope and some fast-energy granola bars, plus whatever else he stuffed secretly into his knapsack. No one was allowed to look into Jerram's things.

She found a sweater for Dad, the kind he liked with a V-neck; and perfume and bath gel for Mom in her favorite scent.

"Are we done?" Grace asked when they collapsed onto one of the wire benches. "We should get a medal for efficiency."

"Almost done. I still have to get you something."

"What are you going to get me?"

"A plaid wool shirt."

Grace laughed. They went up to the food hall and bought some General Tso's chicken at the China Express. Grace searched the tables hopefully, to see if maybe Gregory and Company were around.

"They don't do Christmas shopping," Rose said sympathetically. She thought about Daniel and wondered if she'd get to the point of wanting to buy him shirts.

"You're so contained, Rose," Grace said suddenly.

"What do you mean?"

"You don't get carried away. Like me with Gregory. You've got your mind set on studying dance and that's it. I really admire that."

It was easy to bask in the compliment, but not very honest. Grace was her best friend. "I was just thinking about Daniel, if you want to know the truth."

Grace seemed surprised, then shook her head. "Doesn't matter. You'd never let a guy stand in the way of your career."

It made her sound so calculating. Something inside felt doubtful now. She *had* been self-contained. Until recently. The idea of Daniel was distracting her now.

Some of the foodstalls began to close up, and workers were mopping the floor and stacking chairs. Rose looked at her watch.

"Listen, we'd better call my mom; it's getting late."

By the time her mother arrived it had started to snow. Mom drove home slowly, leaning forward and gripping the wheel the way she always did in bad weather. She was relieved to drop Grace off and get home safely. It made her sort of hyper, and she suggested hot chocolate with whipped cream. Dad was watching television, and Jerram was up in his room.

Rose really didn't want hot chocolate after all the Chinese food but said yes because her mother looked so fluffy and happy as she got out the cream and cocoa.

Jerram came down and had some, too, reading a book and tapping to the beat in his headphones at the same time. Dad came into the kitchen, stretched, sniffed and said where was his.

They sat around the table talking until midnight. Then Mom snapped out of it and cried, "Get to bed!"

Rose felt warm and sleepy. A Totally Contented State, Jerram would probably call it. She slipped effortlessly into sleep without knowing it. And dreamed.

Eight

HER BED WAS AN ISLAND ON AN OCEAN OF FLOOR, or a ship moving slowly toward a distant horizon, the sea as thick and indolent as honey. She sailed for a while, content and undisturbed.

Then she knew something was wrong.

The windows were open. Pine trees glistened in moonlight. Nancy Emerson came in, bringing the fresh clean smell of pine forest with her. No longer was she wearing the piggy-pink down jacket, but was dressed in a long white gown that enveloped her in languid, elegant folds. She floated across the floor.

Again Rose felt annoyed. "Go away!" she growled.

"I've got a problem and I don't know what to do," Nancy said in a practical conversational tone, as if her appearance were nothing unusual, as if she and Rose had just bumped into each other on the street.

"You're dead, Nancy." Rose winced at the harsh truth in the words.

Nancy made a face. "I *know* that," she said,

dismissing it. "But could you come with me a minute?"

Not again, Nancy, Rose wanted to scream, but found herself floating toward the door on the tidal wave that was Nancy's dress. Nancy's clutching hand was cold and dry. Rose could feel the bones inside.

Off the balcony and over the tips of the pines, once again thinking how she had always known how to fly and how she would try it again at Muriel's studio, but be more careful this time.

They flew effortlessly through the night air and this time Rose paid attention. She saw Bethboro below: streetlights winking green and red, the neon glow of the 7-Eleven lighting up a dark corner on route 7, the lights of the Cabin River bridge like a string of diamonds. The recent snow was buttercream frosting on the dark chocolate hills.

I could get into this, she thought, to fly through the night at will, to leave the earth behind, to move upward toward the stars. The wind rushed in her ears, her head felt wild and dizzy. Then Nancy's cold hand tightened and pulled, and they came down to earth with the sickening lurch of a descending roller coaster. There was a bad smell, like lead pencils and erasers ground up in Clorox.

They were in Danville junkyard. Mountains of squashed cars rose up all around, heaps of rusting parts were like an undergrowth. Oily puddles reflected the moonlight. The taste of lead and steel was in Rose's mouth, painfully careening off her fillings.

"What's this all about?" she screamed, her voice the sound of metal rasping against metal.

Nancy pointed. Her long, bony finger went out and reached and reached, beyond the rust and rubber and oil to a stack of sodden deflated tires.

"There," she said.

"What?" Rose strained her eyes, but it was like looking through shadows. "What is it? I don't see anything."

Nancy grabbed and shook her. "There, look, look, why can't you see?" she yelled. "You've got to do something, do something!"

The words rang in Rose's ears as she woke up, as if Nancy had really been in her room, screaming them.

Do what? she thought and felt miserable. Nancy had been found, lifted out of the pine needles, washed and purified, sung to heaven at St. Andrew's church and laid to rest in Bethboro Cemetery. What did she want Rose to do about that? What *could* she do?

Shivering, Rose got up and went into the hall and fished around in the linen closet for the hot-water bottle as quietly as she could. Her mother woke up anyway.

She felt Rose's head for a fever. "I hope you're not coming down with the flu."

Just a bad dream, Mom, she almost replied, but bit her tongue just in time.

Mom filled the hot-water bottle and insisted on tucking Rose back into bed. It made her feel like a little kid, safe and oblivious. It was nice, very cozy.

"Night, Rose," Mom said, kissing her forehead.

"Night, Mom," she whispered drowsily. But as her mother turned away, the folds of her nightdress brushed Rose's hand, and Rose was chilled again by the memory of Nancy's diaphanous robe. The trembling returned full force. It was impossible to recapture that momentary childhood coziness in spite of the hot-water bottle scalding her toes. She couldn't go back to sleep. Now, she was truly afraid.

This was not a coincidence to be rationalized away with Jerram's logic. This was something else. Something very important. How could she explain it? She felt . . . chosen.

Just thinking such a word made her tremble. Whether she liked it or not, whether she knew what to do about it or not, she was being called by the dead . . . to avenge them.

Nine

SHE WOKE FEELING GROGGY AND ON EDGE. GOT dressed and went downstairs fully expecting to hear bad news. Dad woke up to the radio and always gave a news report at breakfast.

He was already at the kitchen table, forcing down the bran cereal he knew was good for him and smelling of the new after-shave Mom had bought him for Christmas but which he'd found before she could hide it. The morning's news was banal: a traffic jam on the Cabin River bridge, a minor fender bender near the mall. No murders or dead bodies, but Rose couldn't shake her gloom. Before the morning was over, she'd snapped at Grace ten times. As always, Grace took it in stride.

"Something's bothering you, Rose. Want to find a quiet place to talk about it at lunch?"

"What, and give up seeing Gregory?" Rose snapped.

"Sure. What's the matter with you?"

None of your business! Rose wanted to yell. Instead, she walked away, not trusting herself to speak.

Grace called after her. "See how you feel at lunch. Remember, nothing's *that* bad."

Oh sure, it's all sweetness and light with you, isn't it? Rose thought. Suddenly she found Grace's goodwill too cloying.

But bad dreams eventually became diluted with the sun. The idea of messages from the dead kept ebbing, finally reduced to only a periodic twinge. Life went on as usual. Gregory and Company got too rowdy in the cafeteria, throwing food, and were given detention. Rose couldn't believe that Daniel had been a part of it, but he caught her eye and winked as he shuffled off with the rest of them in mock obedience. Rose felt her face get hot, and she couldn't bring herself to wink back.

By the end of the day she felt normal again.

"I apologize," she told Grace on the bus. "I'm sorry I was such a grump."

"Don't worry about it," Grace said, but Rose knew she was waiting expectantly to hear why.

"No sleep or something."

Grace nodded. "It's hard to sleep when you have things on your mind," she said invitingly.

"There's nothing much on my mind," Rose said, and Jerram guffawed from the seat behind.

Grace patted her arm in a motherly way. "You were treated badly, Rose. It's natural to feel resentment."

Rose groped around in her mind for what Grace meant. "You mean Detective O'Hara?"

"You were right and she was wrong," Grace said. "You should be mad."

"Thanks, Doc."

"Maybe you can sue."

Rose laughed and felt one hundred percent better. She turned to the window. The hills looked purple and gold, and shafts of afternoon sun glowed on the melting snow along the road. A man wearing a bright plaid deerstalker hat was walking with his dog, both of them puffing in the cold. A tingle of Christmas excitement came over her. It didn't matter that she no longer believed in Santa Claus. She still got excited about Christmas and its traditions. She, Dad and Jerram would go out to Ladyvale Farm and choose the best, most perfect tree. They'd stop at the farm shop for hot cider and doughnuts, and pick out a wreath and a new ornament for the tree from the display of local handicrafts. Last year it had been a small wooden sled with little packages, all wrapped and beribboned. They always waited until Christmas eve to decorate the tree. Mom would insist on messily stringing popcorn and cranberries, just as she'd done as a child. And it would all be accompanied by the soppy Christmas music record, even though they groaned at "Rudolf the Red-nosed Reindeer" and "I Saw Mommy Kissing Santa Claus." It wouldn't be Christmas without it.

A dream is only a dream, Rose thought as she looked at the passing landscape. And at that moment, Nancy's face appeared in the glass, staring at her with eyes red as blood, a twisted mouth screaming in a silent "Help!" Rose stifled her own scream and covered her eyes.

"What's wrong?" Grace asked. Rose forced

herself to look again. Maybe Grace would see it, too?

Nothing there. They were drawing up to the stone house on Fanton Street where the little boy with the hearing aid lived. CAUTION DEAF CHILD, the yellow sign read. No sign of Nancy out there.

Just my own reflection, Rose thought. Some trick of light had turned the window into a mirror. "Something in my eye," she said to Grace. Wasn't that the truth?

She and Jerram got off next, and he moped up the drive behind Rose, earphones on his head, bopping to whatever music was going into his ears. She stopped short, and he bumped into her.

"Give a signal, can't you?" he groused. "What's up?"

"That's what I'd like to know."

Barney was heading toward their kitchen door. Somehow, Barney was always the bearer of bad news.

"Are we going to camp out here or what?" Jerram asked.

"You go on ahead, I'll be there in a minute."

"Take as long as you like, I'm not your mother."

"Jerram, please, just leave me alone."

He shook his head, adjusted his earphones and bopped up the driveway. He and Barney arrived at the kitchen door at the same time. He gave a low bow, held the door open and ushered her in.

There was an insane conversation going on inside Rose's head. I knew it, said a part of her. But a dream is only a dream, said another part.

A dream is not necessarily a dream, said a third.

Rose's toes began to ache. Her toes were her weakness, having been bruised, cracked, lacerated and stunted by toe shoes before Muriel introduced her to modern dance. They hurt in the cold, and they looked ugly. "Monkey toes," Jerram once called them. "Little stubby things like a fringe on the end of your foot."

Suddenly Jerram burst out of the kitchen door, signaling frantically.

I told you so, said her doomsday brain.

She forced her cold toes to walk. Jerram held the door open, saying nothing, only his eyes sparking a hint of excitement.

The kitchen smelled of baking and chocolate. Barney was already stirring the requisite cup of tea Mom always offered. But as Rose came in, it seemed as if everything paused. Barney's spoon stopped stirring. Mom's hand was poised over the box of Sweet 'n Low. Jerram was at the door, frozen in midturn, his hand on the knob.

Then they all began moving. The spoon clattered against the saucer. Mom shoved the box into the cupboard. Jerram slammed the door.

"There's been another one," Barney said eagerly to Rose.

"Another what?"

"Murder, of course."

"We don't know that yet," Mom said testily. "Only that she's disappeared."

Barney shook her head gloomily. "What else could it be?"

"There could be a completely different explanation. We might all be jumping to conclusions."

"A serial killer, that's what it is," Barney pronounced.

"What kind? Cornflakes? Cheerios? Granola Crunch?" Jerram quipped.

Barney was annoyed at such levity when she was trying so hard to keep the atmosphere somber. "Mark my words," she intoned.

"We've never had any trouble like this before," Mom said. "I can't believe this could happen a second time."

"Why should Bethboro be exempt from violence?" Jerram asked.

"That kind of talk does no good," Mom said. "This is a nice town, with nice people in it."

"Okay, Mom, okay."

"Who was . . . *is* it?" Rose asked.

"One of Nancy's friends," Barney said, and Rose felt her heart thud. Nancy would be worried about her friend, would want somebody to help.

"A girl from Beacon Street," Mom put in. "And to think you and Grace just walked there yesterday, on your way to the mall."

There was silence for a moment as each of them thought their own thoughts.

"Of course, they think it might be suicide," Barney offered, as if she realized nobody wanted to go on talking about murder. Everybody looked at her as she took a sip of tea, savoring the moment. "Depression, you know?" she said in a low voice as if it were something immoral. "They think she was depressed over Nancy's death.

They say kids do copycat things like that."

"Who the heck is *they*?" Jerram asked belligerently, making Mom frown.

Barney looked ruffled. "People in charge, of course."

Mom seemed to like this theory. "Maybe you're right. Nancy's friend could have been terribly upset."

"Oh, yes, it happens all the time," Barney said. "More than likely. There's only a one-in-a-million chance for another murder happening here, so soon after the other."

"That's what I think," Mom agreed. She was warming to the subject.

Rose had to get out of the kitchen. "I'm sick of all this," she said ungraciously.

She could hear their voices behind her, whispery and full of concern. "It must be upsetting for her; they were girls from school," Mom was saying.

"She needs therapy," Barney advised.

"Give her a break, can't you?" Jerram said.

She locked herself in her room and wouldn't answer even when Jerram knocked. He called to her, then she heard him muttering as he went away.

But the room wasn't much of a haven now; it felt contaminated with the dreams, yet it was the only place she had to be alone.

She thought for a long time, until the sun went twinking down and night fell. Would the police find Nancy's friend in Danville junkyard? Did it matter, since she was dead, anyway? But it wasn't fair for people to start believing she had committed suicide. She deserved to be found, if only for that.

"Do something!" Nancy had said.

Rose knew she had to.

Ten

SHE HAD NO TIME TO MAKE PEANUT BUTTER cookies. But she packed a slab of the chocolate cake Mom had made that afternoon and sneaked out of the house. Only Jerram knew where she was going, and he had eagerly agreed to cover for her by pretending they were working together in his room. "I'm glad you're doing this," he said. "And that you're trusting me."

"Why wouldn't I trust you?"

"I mean, we're doing this together, aren't we? Just the two of us. Like our old secrets. No outsiders."

"No outsiders," Rose agreed and wondered if Jerram knew she had considered calling Daniel to ask him to go with her. She'd actually looked up his telephone number but hadn't been able to bring herself to dial it. She wasn't ready to tell Daniel about these things yet.

She got on her bike and started toward North Hill. It was more of a mountain than a hill. Halfway there she had to stop and walk the bike.

The wind was cold and pushy, blowing down from the top. It started to sleet, and she could hardly see where she was going. She thought of that crazy music, *Night on Bald Mountain.* Not something you could hum, but it fit the bill. She felt like the only one alive in the world.

At last she reached Old Mackey's house. It sat, squat and secretive behind tall hedges, a meager light burning on the porch, a dim glow coming from behind the curtains across the window of one room. She racked the bike against the porch railing and knocked on the door. After a long wait, a gravelly voice shouted, "Well? Are you coming in or not?"

She pushed, and the old door creaked open. The hall was dark. A cat came out from the only lighted room and inspected her, sniffing along the edges of her wet boots. Dimly, she could see a man in the next room, sitting in a chair with a book in his hands. She dripped off, gaining courage, and removed the foil-wrapped package from her pocket before hanging her coat on the rack amid an odd assortment of jackets, coats and scarves.

"Hello?" Rose ventured, "Mr. Mackey?" She made sure to pronounce it right. He got up from the chair then, leaning on a cane. Peered out and gave a sniff much like the cat had. Rose stepped forward and proffered the foil-wrapped cake. He took it with his free hand.

"It's homemade, with real butter."

"Thank you," he said and sat down. He put the package on the table next to his chair, picked up the book he had been reading when she arrived and resumed reading it now.

Rose stood there, uncertainly. The cat came around from behind a chair in the corner and stared at her.

Mackey looked up from his book. "You still here?"

"I guess so."

"Either you are or you aren't."

"I am."

Mackey showed no inclination to put his book aside. She needed to do something drastic.

"I have a confession to make."

He raised his eyebrows.

"That cake was a bribe."

He looked interested.

"I have to tell you something. Something I know about something that's happened."

He lifted his arm to take in the room. "This isn't the police station, love."

"I've already been there, they wouldn't listen to me. Well, not the first time anyway. I can't go back again."

"Commit some crime, did you?" He laid the book aside.

"I'll try to explain."

He sighed. "Aye, well, sit down if it's going to be a long story."

Her story came out awkwardly. As if listening intently, the cat crept closer and then jumped into her lap. She stroked its back, and it started to purr.

"Watch out," Mackey said. "It's a fickle creature."

"Mr. Mackey, do you think it sounds crazy?"

"I can't say off the top of my head. I'll have to think about it."

The cat stopped purring and abruptly smacked Rose with a sharp claw. Rose rubbed at the tiny droplets of blood.

"Bad puss," Mackey said abstractedly.

It was quiet in the room. Eventually Rose could make out the individual sounds of the house: the faint ticking of a clock, a tap dripping and what she guessed must be heat moving through the pipes like a flushed toilet.

"Will you take a cup of tea?" he asked. "It's a nasty night to have come out."

He stood up, found his cane and hobbled off, refusing an offer of help. Rose and the cat stared at each other with mutual malice while he was gone.

There was a clattering in the kitchen, then he brought in a teapot and took fragile china cups and saucers from an old china cabinet. Rose knew then it was a special occasion and that old Mackey did not often have visitors. He was enjoying himself. Perhaps he didn't believe her at all. They drank tea and ate the chocolate cake. At last, Mackey spoke. "I do not believe in ghosts, but neither do I disbelieve in them."

She told him she had not thought of Nancy as a ghost.

"A ghost might appear in a dream or not as it sees fit. Perhaps she didn't want to scare you."

"But she did. This time at least. I'm usually a sensible person," Rose added lamely.

"A relief that is," he said. "Too many people without sense in this world."

"Then you believe me?"

He put up his hand. "*Vigilate et orate,*" he said. "Watch and pray. In the meantime, what do you want from me?"

It was an unexpected question. What did she want? "I thought if you believed me, *you'd* know what to do."

"Have a word with the police on your behalf?"

"Yes, something like that. They'd listen to you."

"Tell them about this little chat?"

"No!"

Mackey looked serious. "It's never wise to mask the truth. If this girl is found where you say she is, God help her, there will be a police investigation. Your part in it may have to come out."

"But could you not say anything at first? It could turn out to be nothing at all. And if they don't find any . . . thing . . . in the junkyard, then nobody needs to know about my dream."

"You don't like the gift then?"

"What gift?"

"The second sight."

Rose felt a tremor go through her.

"No, I can see not," Mackey said sadly. "It's a heavy burden for a young girl like yourself."

"You really believe in things like that?"

"Didn't you already suspect as much? Why else would you come to see Old Mackey?"

"My brother told me to come."

"Ah, now I place you. That naughty young man's sister. He's grown up considerably since we first met. Comes up here for a chat quite regularly. And has he the gift as well?"

"I don't know," Rose said slowly, trying to absorb the fact that Jerram made a habit of visiting Mackey. She'd thought it was just that once, years ago on Halloween. The idea that Jerram had kept it a secret was something new, to be considered later. "We used to think we had the same dreams, but that may be natural with twins."

"'Sleep hath its own world, and a wide realm of wild reality,'" Mackey said. "'And dreams in their development have breath, and tears, and tortures and the touch of joy.'"

They were silent for a moment. Sleet slashed against Mackey's windows.

"Will you help?" Rose asked timidly.

"I'll think on it and do what I can. But for now, it's time you were getting back home. Will your parents be picking you up?"

"No, I have my bike. I'll be fine."

Mackey looked disapproving and pursed his lips as he opened the door and looked out at the weather. "Perhaps it's clearing a wee bit," he said doubtfully. The cat peered out into the darkness and sneezed.

"Godspeed," Mackey called from the doorway as Rose rode away.

But the road was too slick to keep riding, and the sleet cut her eyes and turned her nose to ice. The only good thing was that it was all downhill. She was nearly home when she noticed the headlights. She moved over to the shoulder of the road, but the car stayed behind her, moving almost at the same pace. She panicked, thinking it was Dad out searching, but for a time the car never came closer. She could see better in its headlights, but it made her nervous, afraid to move out into the road in case she got run down. Finally the car accelerated. When it was parallel with her, it slowed to a crawl and whoever was driving reached over to swipe at the steamy window, as if to get a good look at her. She could see now it wasn't Dad or Mom, or even Barney. But it might be someone who'd recognize her, who might say something. Rose turned her head away. The car hovered, then passed, only to slow down again beyond the intersection. Luckily it was her cross street, and she turned and hurried up the block to the house.

She managed to sneak upstairs without being seen. Mom and Dad were watching television. Jerram was waiting in his room.

"You look like a drowned rat," he said. "Take a hot shower, and I'll bring you some tea with lemon."

He sat next to her on the bed as she drank it and told him what had transpired at Mackey's.

"Mackey will help, you'll see," Jerram said when she'd finished.

Two things were bothering her. The idea of Jerram's regular visits to Mackey, and the question the old man had asked about Jerram having the gift, too. Inside of her there had been this growing suspicion that Jerram wasn't telling her the truth about the dreams. But she'd told herself she was wrong, Jerram and she shared everything. Now, knowing that they didn't, she felt the suspicion welling up again.

"Jerram, is it true that you haven't dreamed

about Nancy? You've got to tell me."

He looked undecided, then reluctantly shook his head. "I wish I had. Then we'd be like before, a united front. I don't know why it isn't happening anymore." He looked crushed.

Rose felt guilty for having doubted him. "You couldn't dream anyway, could you? You never sleep," she joked tiredly to cover up her feelings.

"We vampires have too much to do at night, in the dark. . . ." he said in his Count Dracula voice, then stopped. "Hey, Rose, lighten up."

"It's hard. I hope they don't find the girl in the junkyard. I don't even know her name. Do you?"

"Cyn. For Cynthia."

"What good are these dreams, anyway? They never give me any real information like names and phone numbers."

"You did get more this time than last, though. Old Nancy is getting smarter. She gave you the coordinates. You know exactly where it is. I guess she just needed practice."

Rose hit him with a pillow. "Maybe it's just me who needed practice. Actually, I was paying more attention this time. I could see us flying over the 7-Eleven toward Danville, and so it had to be that big auto junk place out on route 7."

"Mac's going to tell them to look there?"

Rose nodded. "He told me to watch and pray. And he spouted something about sleep being a realm of wild reality. It wasn't very comforting."

Jerram stood up and struck a theatrical pose. " 'To sleep, perchance to dream . . .' " he began. Mom came in at that moment. Jerram froze, then laughed. Mom laughed and said it was time for bed and then stopped short, seeing Rose already tucked in.

"I knew it," she said. "You're coming down with something."

"Mom, I was just a little tired."

She looked unconvinced. "Mark my words," she said, sounding like Barney, "a mother knows these things."

"ESP runs rampant in this family," Jerram said. "No wonder Dad does so well in the stock market."

He said good night, and Mom followed him out, nagging about some mess he'd left in the living room.

Rose pulled the covers up to her chin, noticing the angry red mark on her hand where Mackey's cat had smacked her. She probably didn't like him having visitors. Jealous old lady; she'd been gray around her whiskers and chin. Rose wondered how it would be to live alone on North Hill with a cupboard full of translucent teacups and pipes that sounded like the ocean, sitting in a chair all day and spouting Latin to a cat.

About all she could do was *vigilate et orate*. Watch to see whether they found Cynthia. Pray to have no more dreams.

She was almost asleep with the light still on when Jerram came back. "Mom says you're supposed to smear this on your chest," he said.

"Just stick it on the table," she said.

He put the blue jar of Vicks down and hesitated.

"Are you going to stand there, checking?"

"No, no, it's all the same to me whether you get Vapo-rubbed or not. No, I meant to tell you before. You got a phone call while you were out. I grabbed the phone quick, before Mom could."

"Okay." Rose felt half asleep.

"It was the dingdong."

Rose opened her eyes and felt awake again. "You're being really rude, Jerram."

"All right, it was Daniel."

"What did he say?"

"He asked to talk to you."

"What did you tell him?"

"That you were out, that you wouldn't be in till way late."

"Oh, God."

"I was polite, Rose, I mean it. I didn't call him dingdong."

"He'll think I had a date or something."

"So?"

"So, I'd rather that he didn't think so, that's all!"

"*C'est la vie,*" Jerram said, sounding unworried, and he went out and shut the door.

Rose let herself fantasize. Maybe it had been Daniel in the car, out looking for her? Then she sat bolt upright in bed. Was she crazy? Nancy was dead, and Cynthia was missing, and she had been followed tonight. Maybe it had been *him*?

No, of course it hadn't been. Just some nosy busybody. Because otherwise, she wouldn't be here in bed, safe.

How lovely it would be to go back in time. Be a little kid whose only worries were the bogeyman in the closet and the monsters under the bed. The cat scratch throbbed, and she licked it. Could you get rabies from a scratch? No, Mackey's cat would never have rabies; she was a police cat.

Down, down she went into sleep. Slept and dreamed, but these were fine dreams, of cats sailing the ocean in bobbing teacups painted with roses. On the far shore, someone waited, and she hoped it might be Daniel.

In the morning she woke up with the flu, just as her mother had predicted.

Part Three

Him

I MISSED AN OPPORTUNITY TONIGHT. PERHAPS this one has some power that makes her strong. I will keep my eye on her. She is worth watching.

Sometimes I think how amusing it would be if Santa in his sleigh threw down packages of dead flesh upon the world.

Piece on earth, peace on earth, bad will to them.

Rose

Eleven

FOR TWO OR THREE DAYS ROSE LIVED IN THE dreams of a high fever. But by Tuesday morning, she had come back to reality. Mom immediately presented her with her schoolbooks and all the homework assignments Jerram had dutifully brought home. Just when she was looking forward to a tubercular-type convalescence, languishing on the couch, watching the soaps all afternoon.

She wasn't in the mood for schoolwork. She wanted to talk to Grace and find out if Cyn's body had been found.

Mom wouldn't say anything. She only made soothing noises when Rose tried to ask. Don't concern yourself with such things when you're ill, she said, and in the next breath told her to get on with her homework.

At lunch, Mom noticed her glances at the wall clock. "Got an appointment?" she joked.

"Just want to talk to Grace. Catch up on what's been happening."

Did a shadow cross Mom's face? She felt a now-familiar sinking sensation in the pit of her stomach. There was no doubt but that Cyn's body had turned up. Otherwise Mom would have been broadcasting the good news.

Rose went back to bed and fell asleep soundly until she heard the phone ringing at around four o'clock. It was already getting dark outside — the day had slipped away.

She got out of bed, felt a little shaky and dizzy and went to the top of the stairs.

Mom was saying, "She's asleep, Grace. Why don't you try again later?"

"It's okay, Mom, I've got it," she said, picking up the hall extension. She waited to hear the click of Mom's hanging up.

"Hi."

Grace didn't waste time. "You'll never guess. Gregory asked me for a date! A date, Rose, did you hear me?"

"That's really great."

"Can you believe it?"

"Not really. Did you say yes?"

"Of course I said yes, what else would I say?"

"No?"

"Why would I say that? Oh, listen, Rose, I'm sorry. How are you feeling? I missed you. I tried calling Sunday and yesterday but your mom said you were really sick."

"Raving with fever, but I'm a lot better now."

"Then I guess you didn't hear. They found a skeleton in the Danville junkyard. They think it's a girl, and she was murdered."

"And it was Cynthia, right? Nancy Emerson's friend who'd disappeared?"

"No, I told you, it was a *skeleton*. It'd been there for years. Nobody knows who it is."

Rose couldn't take it in at first. A skeleton? What did Nancy have to do with a skeleton? And where was her friend Cyn?

". . . acting like there's a murderer around every corner," Grace was saying. "Real paranoia time. But now I'm so nervous about Gregory. I'm like, my God, I'm going on a date with him! I'm beginning to wish it was like before, when he just wouldn't talk to me. I mean, he doesn't talk to me now, either, which is weird when you think this Friday we're going to be alone. I hope he talks then because I think I'm gonna clam up."

"Have they found Cynthia?"

"Who's Cynthia? Oh, are you still on that? Please don't you get morbid like everyone else in town. Rose? Rose! Tell me it isn't true . . . you had another one of those dreams?"

She tried to laugh. "You get some crazy dreams when you have 104 fever."

"So where is she?" Grace asked in a hushed voice.

"I have no idea."

"No idea, huh? Well, if you don't want to tell me . . ." Grace sounded hurt. The date with Gregory really was making her a nervous wreck.

"No, really. I did have a dream but it was about that . . . that skeleton. I'm scared."

"It is scary. But *you* never seemed to be scared of talking about entities and stuff like this before. I never wanted to meet up with any entities, but you used to think it would be a great idea."

It had been easy to talk about those things when they were only theoretical. "This is different. It's really happening."

"Well, there's one comfort. You were too sick to tell the police. At least you won't have to go through that again."

"Maybe . . . I don't know." She told Grace about the trip to see Mackey.

"And you get the flu for your trouble. I don't know why you bothered."

"Because of Nancy. She made me. It seemed so important to her."

"Yeah, but Nancy's dead and it wasn't her friend they found."

"I know. It's strange. Maybe it means Cyn is alive."

"Everybody's still looking for her. If Nancy knows so much, why send you to a skeleton that's been buried for years?" Grace was getting upset now. "And what is she picking on you for? Why not just tattletale to her parents or better still, go to the police direct?"

"I've asked myself that question a hundred times. All I come up with is the fact that I was nice to her when she was having that problem last year, whatever it was."

"That makes her life sound pretty bleak. Wasn't anybody else ever nice to her?"

"Or maybe she picked me because I'm the only one she can reach."

"Listen, Rose, if she can come back from the dead she can certainly pick and choose who she talks to."

Grace's words gave Rose a sense of relief. "You don't think it's because I have some kind of special power that nobody else has?"

"I don't think it has anything to do with special powers. Nancy's doing it for some dumb reason of her own. She always was a pain."

"How do you know that?"

"Well . . . she seemed the type. It's probably a sin to be talking bad about the dead, but next time she comes along, tell her to buzz off."

"Next time? I hope there is no next time."

"Oh, me, too. I didn't realize how that sounded, you know what I mean."

Remembering what Barney had said in the kitchen last week, about serial killers and suicides, Rose asked, "You don't think these things could be connected, do you? Nancy's murder and the skeleton and Cyn?"

"Probably not. Anyway, whoever or whatever, it'll be all right. This isn't New York, people can't get away with bad stuff here."

"But there must be some kind of connection with Nancy. Otherwise why would she give me messages about an old skeleton?"

"Who knows what dead people think."

"Grace, do you realize how bizarre this is? The way we're talking about Nancy?"

"Well, there really are psychics who help the police solve murders. You're nutty enough to be one, Rose. No, only fooling. I don't have any explanations. Let's just forget it, as you once said not too long ago."

"Yeah. It's more interesting to talk about Gregory and Company, right?"

"Not *and Company*, if you don't mind. I hope he's not planning to bring Randy, Paul and Daniel along on our date. By the way, Daniel was asking about you."

"He was?" Why didn't he just call, Rose thought, with disappointment, if he wanted to know how I was?

Mom appeared at the top of the stairs. "Rose, are you still on that phone? Look at you, standing there without your slippers."

"Gotta go, Grace."

"I heard. See ya soon."

Rose was hustled back to bed. Mom said she'd bring up chicken soup for supper.

"Where's Jerram?"

"I think he went to the health club after school."

"You *think* he went?"

"He might have gone to Westley. He has some friend there. Whatever, he promised to be back by six."

A friend in Westley? Who could that be? Rose couldn't remember any friend of Jerram's living over there. She wriggled away from Mom's fussing hands that were smoothing the bedclothes. She started to feel angry.

"You're not worried about him? Aren't you going to pick him up?"

"What for?" Mom said, fluffing the pillows in

spite of Rose's protests. "He can take care of himself."

"That's sexism, Mom."

Mom stopped fussing. "It's not boys who are getting themselves killed around here." She looked as if she regretted the words, then sighed. "I suppose Grace told you."

"About the skeleton. But it doesn't have anything to do with the murder, does it?"

Mom looked at her. "Well, it's obvious it was *another* murder. People who die natural deaths don't get buried in the Danville dump!" she cried.

Rose took a deep breath. "I know you're worried, Mom. But here I am, safe and sound in bed. Why can't we just talk about it rationally?"

"Because murder isn't rational!"

"But don't treat me like a baby."

"I know you're not a baby. But I don't like talking about these things."

"You wish it would all go away," Rose said, and she could hear the accusation in her voice. But she was really accusing herself, wishing her dreams away.

"And why not? What's wrong with a mother wishing for her daughter's safety?"

"Nobody's going to get me, Mom."

Suddenly Rose needed to talk about Jerram. Why were they growing apart? "Mom?"

"Yes?"

But Rose found she couldn't put it into words. It was hard enough to put it into thoughts.

"Nothing."

Horrible as it was to admit, she was starting to

distrust Jerram. Why couldn't it be the way it used to be between them, when they'd stuck together, shared their thoughts and dreams. Now he was so secretive: visits to Mackey, a friend in Westley, maybe even dreams. What if he was keeping his own dreams of Nancy a secret?

It felt as if a part of her were being torn away, slowly, with a lot of bleeding. She and Jerram were separating, becoming different. All her life, Jerram had been her counterpart, her reflection, her other half.

If Jerram's thoughts ceased to be her thoughts, if her dreams ceased to be his, then a big hole would form inside of her where Jerram had been. Black, empty, cold . . . it would make her vulnerable, like a door left open. And what if Nancy tried to get in? What if Nancy wanted to take Jerram's place, as a sort of doppelgänger, to become the other, deathly half of her?

Twelve

JERRAM BROUGHT A NEWSPAPER UP TO HER ROOM when he came home. The discovery of the skeleton was on the front page. It had been determined to be the remains of an adolescent female between the ages of fourteen and eighteen. They were going to try to identify her by her teeth.

"Do skeletons have teeth?" Rose wondered.

"Complete with fillings. They can find out who it is by comparing dental records."

"But how do they know which dentist to ask?"

"Start around here, I guess. Except that no girl that age was reported missing in the last five years. That's how long they think the thing's been there."

"I wonder who it could be."

"Of course, they haven't included *all* the gory details. Like bloodstains, or if any flesh was left on the bones or any hair left on her head."

"Jerram, please! The poor girl."

"She doesn't care anymore. The time to worry about her was before she was murdered."

"I guess it *was* murder?"

"Looks pretty sure. Fractured skull, broken ribs."

"She could be from miles away," Rose said. "The body could have been buried there by killers from someplace else."

"They'll figure it out eventually," Jerram said. "In the meantime, you're not supposed to be reading about it. So hide the paper if Mom comes in."

"No, I won't. She keeps treating me like a baby. It's okay for you to walk home alone, but I've got to be chauffeured around and protected from a newspaper!" She spread the paper ostentatiously across the bed. "And where were you this afternoon, anyway?" she snapped.

Jerram was surprised. "Working out at the health club, why?"

She peered up at him. Was that the truth? Or had he been over in Westley, or up at Mackey's? "Never mind."

He sat down on the end of the bed and touched her feet through the blankets. "Poor old monkey toes," he said. "You can't blame Mom. You girls like to think you're equal and all that but it's girls who're getting murdered, not boys."

"I don't like the sound of 'you girls.'"

"Anyway, you forgot how they wouldn't let me go on that spelunking expedition two years ago. Of course, I went on my own at another time," he added smugly.

"A troglodyte like you could never get lost in a cave."

Jerram hunched his back and made a horrible face. He walked around the room making snuffling sounds and finally got her to laugh.

"I wish I had a cat," she said suddenly, and Jerram stopped clowning around.

"Why?"

"Maybe I need something to cuddle," she replied, realizing just how true that might be.

"I'd rather have a wolf," Jerram said. "A white wolf who runs like the wind. I'd change myself into a wolf, too, at the full moon and race with him."

"And they'd shoot you with a silver bullet. Seriously, I feel so alone."

"You've got me, kid," Jerram said.

"Do I? It's not the same between us, and you know it. Especially since you started acting so weird."

"I've always been weird."

"I'm serious," Rose said, determined to get it out now. "Okay, maybe secretive is the better word. You have secrets now. You never had them before."

He gave her a long look. "You have secrets, too, Rose," he said quietly.

"Yeah, like what?" she threw back at him. "I've told you everything, all about the dreams, Nancy. . . ."

"Secrets like Daniel."

Rose was shocked. "He's not a secret."

"No? So how come I never heard of him until he starts calling the house every five minutes?"

"What are you talking about. You know Daniel, you see him every day."

"I mean you never told me about him and you."

"There is no him or me. I mean, not yet. There was nothing to tell." Why should she feel guilty all of a sudden? What was he doing to her mind? "And he hasn't called every five minutes. Just once last week."

Jerram's face flushed, and he got up and went over to the window. "Well, that's not exactly true. He called when you were sick. You were in no shape to talk, you know. I guess . . . I forgot."

Rose didn't know whether to believe him. But he really did look repentant and embarrassed. And the fact was that Jerram did often forget phone messages. Mom was always nagging him to write them down.

She knew he was waiting for the magic words. "Okay. I forgive you. Just this once."

He smiled. "Not to change the subject," he said, and of course did. "But I've been thinking. What if this new body is connected to Nancy Emerson and her friend Cyn? Maybe it's a serial killer, like Barney said. We all laugh at her crackpot ideas, but it's too much to believe that three murders in Bethboro are coincidence."

"Maybe. But we don't know about Cyn."

"Cold-blooded as it sounds, let's assume she's dead, too."

"It could have been suicide, like Barney also said."

He shook his head. "Suicides don't bury themselves so well. Cyn would have swallowed pills or done something close to home. Even if she jumped off the Cabin River bridge they'd have found her body. I think she was abducted, just like Nancy, in a car. The skeleton was found in an auto junkyard which, again, indicates use of a car. Somebody out there is cruising, looking for victims."

Rose remembered the car that followed her the night she went to see Mackey. Had she been so close to danger? "But the skeleton doesn't have to be related; it's five years old. Why would someone wait five years between murders?"

"Who says he did? Who says these are the only bodies? They're just the ones that have been found."

"God, is this going to go on forever? If I'm going to be cursed with this psychic 'gift,' as Mackey calls it, what good does it do for me to find dead bodies?"

"Get 'em while they're fresh, with plenty of clues, it could lead to the killer," Jerram said heartlessly.

"But why not just lead me to the killer in the first place?"

"Interesting question," Jerram said excitedly. He sat down on the bed again. "You sure you haven't seen anything else in the dreams?"

"Just what I told you." She thought a moment. "Maybe the dead can only speak of the dead. I mean, maybe Nancy's powers are limited."

"You're looking green, Rose."

"Just feeling a little queasy. Mom's supposed to be bringing me chicken soup in a minute."

"That'll cure you. I'll go see if it's ready." He went to call down the stairs but Mom was just coming up.

Rose left the newspaper on the bed, and Mom made a show of ignoring it as she put the tray down on Rose's knees.

"I could come down to supper," Rose said.

"You've got a stubborn streak," Mom said, not unkindly. "I can't imagine where you got it." It was her way of lightening it up, making a joke, because everyone knew Dad always called Mom stubborn herself.

Jerram went downstairs to eat. It was only when Rose was contentedly slurping hot chicken broth and crunching toast that she realized she'd never gotten back to Jerram's secrets. They'd only talked about Rose and Daniel and the murders. She was sure Jerram had fixed it that way, as if he didn't want to be asked questions.

She got sick of being sick and coddled and protected. The next morning she wobbled downstairs, fully dressed and determined to go to school. Mom tried to dissuade her, but Dad and Jerram were on her side. Dad said part of growing up was to learn your limitations, and you couldn't find out what they were unless you gave yourself a try. Jerram said he'd keep an eye out and rush her to the school nurse at the first sign of trouble. Mom relented and Rose went off, fortified with herb tea liberally laced with honey and a piece of dry toast in her stomach. As she stepped outside, the air was like a cold slap in the face. She flinched and forced in a breath, remembering Dad's speech on limitations.

"I hope you didn't mean that," she said to

Jerram, trying not to shiver. "About watching me all day."

"Probably not," he admitted. "But do me a favor and promise you'll take yourself to the nurse if you feel a relapse coming on. I don't want to damage my reputation as steadfast older brother."

"Older by five minutes!"

"I got here first, doesn't matter by how much."

The bus lumbered to a stop, its tires crunching the light crust of newly fallen snow. The door opened with a pneumatic hiss. "Age before beauty," Rose said and waved Jerram up the steps first.

There was no need for worry. Grace took over as nursemaid, guiding Rose by the elbow from class to class, keeping everybody else at bay. After feeling unpleasantly cold on the bus Rose felt horribly hot in school.

"You could go home, you know," Grace said. "You look awful."

"Thanks."

"Maybe you have a fever." She tried to feel Rose's forehead.

"Lay off!" Rose snapped. It wasn't just getting over the flu, it was something going on inside that had nothing to do with being sick. A gnawing sensation, as if she'd forgotten something extremely important and remembering it was a matter of life or death. She tried to apologize, but Grace said not to worry about it, she understood. Her understanding only made Rose feel crankier.

At lunch she said she didn't want to sit near Gregory and Company. She didn't want Daniel looking at her red nose and sweaty face. Grace looked relieved instead of disappointed. "He still hasn't said a word to me," she confided. "I hope he remembers to show up for our date."

"You're sure he really made a date?" Rose asked. And when Grace looked confused, she plunged ahead. "I mean, it wasn't a figment of your airhead imagination?"

It took a lot to make Grace angry. In fact, in all the years of friendship, Grace probably hadn't been angry more than twice, and that was only when they were kids fighting about sharing toys. But now her face darkened in a way Rose had never seen before. Her lips became a tight line. Rose knew she'd overstepped the mark. The funny thing was, she couldn't care. The gnawing had grown into something frightening inside her and she felt as if she might explode.

Grace methodically continued eating her lunch with lowered eyes. Rose watched her sticking the tines of the fork into a piece of gooy mayonnaise-covered chicken, raising the fork to her mouth, sticking the chicken in between her lips, chewing, swallowing. It was the most disgusting sight she'd ever seen. She wanted to grab Grace by the hair and shove her face down into the plate.

"Gotta go to the bathroom," she mumbled and rushed away from the table. She had to get out of there fast, before the demon inside her made her do something terrible.

It *was* like a demon. Like something inside her

body, a pressure building and building.

She went to the basement ladies' room where nobody ever hung out at lunchtime and shut herself in one of the stalls. She sat there, just trying to catch her breath.

The pressure was like a festering noise now, building to a deafening crescendo.

"What do you want?" she shouted, not caring if anyone came in and heard. There was no answer. Only the small sound of one of the faucets dripping.

And then the smell.

Something decaying, putrid. A rancid yet sweet smell of blood that she could almost taste.

This is how it is to be dead, she thought. This is how the dead feel if they could feel. The body rotting from the inside out, brittle bones, translucent jelly flesh, the brain festering, the skull pressing against the stretched skin of the face, trying to break through and grin.

Faintly something was saying it was sorry, it hadn't meant to do this, it was all a mistake. But the slow death continued, and Rose could hear the moaning winds of limbo. She was putrefying.

The bathroom door opened and in spite of her fear at what was happening, she felt embarrassed, worrying that whoever was coming in would think she'd caused the foul smell that now hung in the room like a dense fog.

Hesitant footsteps. Then Grace's voice. "Rose? You in here?"

She drew her feet up so they wouldn't be visible under the stall door. But Grace rattled the door.

"Excuse me, but is that you in there, Rose?"

The smell was all Rose could think of, how terrible, how humiliating.

"Answer me, Rose! Jerram is worried, too."

She opened her mouth, in good faith, she wanted to say something, but nothing came out.

"I'm gonna get somebody," Grace said.

Rose made a sound, like something a half-dead animal might make, a death gurgle. She unlocked the door with fingers that felt swollen with fetid blood.

"Sorry," her skullhead said for her. "I don't know where that smell is coming from. I mean, I was only sitting here thinking."

Grace was looking at her with grave concern. "What smell? What are you babbling about?"

"Can't you smell it? The stink of death."

"You have a fever. You need to go home."

"You think I'm delirious. Maybe I am. Something weird is going on inside." Rose clutched her arm.

Grace was alarmed but kept her head. She helped Rose out to the hall where Jerram was waiting.

"Why didn't you come in, too?" Rose asked and laughed. "Since when do you stand on ceremony?"

Jerram and Grace exchanged glances.

"Rose," Jerram said, taking her face in his hands. "We're going to take you home, okay?"

"I think we should call an ambulance," Grace said.

Jerram didn't think so. They stopped and had a debate about who to call; Mom, Dad, an ambulance, the school nurse. Rose leaned against the wall, observing it all as if from a thousand miles away. Oddly, she began to feel better. Whatever had been inside her was easing itself out, and the fresh air of life was blowing back in.

"Hey, listen," she tried to say.

Grace's head seemed to swivel on her neck. She grinned at Rose, and blackened lips worked with greenish spittle as some words croaked out. "Look in Ladyvale Caves," the cadaverous mouth said. And then suddenly it was Grace again, asking if she was okay.

Rose heard herself wailing from far off, "This isn't fair." She was vaguely aware of someone else appearing and of Jerram turning on this person and telling him to mind his own business and go away. "Wait," Rose said weakly. She was sure the person was Daniel. But all she could make out was a retreating back. How embarrassing to have made such a scene. What would he think of her now?

Someone must have made a phone call because after she had been wrapped up in her sweaters and coat, they took her right out to Mom's waiting car.

"Don't worry, it's just a high fever," the school nurse was saying, and she tucked Rose into the car.

"I knew this would happen," Mom complained in accusing tones. "I don't know why you insisted on going to school." Rose was familiar with this way of Mom's handling anxiety, scolding or nagging when she cared most.

"I'll be okay."

"You certainly will when I get you into bed."

"Yes, Mom." Rose was relaxing. It had been a dumb idea to go to school. She thought of her warm bed, of going to sleep. A fever was bound to make you a little crazy. A fever could give you all kinds of nutty ideas and after all, death had been on her mind lately. Delirious was the word.

As Mom drove the car away from the school, Rose looked back to wave. To see if maybe Daniel had reappeared; to make it up to Grace. Poor Grace. She'd been a real bitch to her.

Grace and Jerram were standing in front of the glass doors, watching the car. In front of them was Nancy, dressed up in her stupid white angel dress.

You're going to freeze in that, Rose thought.

Unwillingly, she raised her hand in acknowledgment, knowing there was nothing she could do about it. She'd have to tell someone about Ladyvale Caves because that was where they'd find Cyn for sure. She was in Nancy's power now; Nancy had given her a taste of death.

She waved. Nancy smiled and waved back.

Part Four

Him

I HAD BEEN SAVING THIS ONE UP FOR A CHRISTMAS treat but I had to get rid of her. She talked too much. I had to wrap her up like a Christmas present to keep her quiet.

She can sleep now. Peace in sleep. Sleepful peace. Death loves her. Anyway, it was getting too hard to hide her. A risk I should not take again. Wollenschaft could get suspicious. I have always been a careful person, which is why I have been able to hide this long.

It is the season of tradition, the season of jolly, joyous blood. It makes me remember the other Christmas and I feel sad, angry, hateful things. Killing helps. And it might be a good idea to send some greeting to them all in this town of my sister. It is joyous blood season and I have a right to be happy, too. She who is my sister is walking around living. This I will not tolerate forever.

Silent Night.

Rose

Thirteen

LADYVALE CAVES ARE IN THE LAUREL HILLS beyond Ladyvale Farm, in the western uplands of Connecticut. They're not much of a challenge for a real spelunker, just ordinary boulder caves formed by the collapse of the cliff face, small and narrow with an occasional strange rock formation. But they can be dangerous, and every few years there's a campaign to prevent kids from going up there, and the newspaper runs a protest piece on how the graffiti inside the caves is ruining the area's national heritage.

That's where Cyn was found.

She'd been stabbed, just like Nancy Emerson, but also strangled; her scarf knotted tight around her neck. They found her after Mackey gave Rose's message to Chief Henning.

Rose had asked Jerram to deliver the message to Mackey. When Mom brought her home from school, she'd had a 104° fever and could hardly talk. Dr. Morris made a house call, a real miracle. By the time Jerram got home from school she was halfway human and was able to tell him what he had to do.

He looked at her long and hard and then turned away and punched the wall with his fist. And when that made too much noise and threatened to leave a dent, he began punching the end of her bed.

She felt afraid. "It's bad, isn't it, my getting these messages from the dead? It makes me feel dirty."

"It has nothing to do with you." He scowled, then his face softened. "I mean, no, there's nothing shameful about it, and that's not why I'm upset." He was silent. She had to urge him to go on.

"Why you, Rose? Why only *you*? It's been eating at me. I know it's stupid, but I can't help it."

"I've been asking myself the same question."

He smiled sadly. "You want to know the truth? I feel jealous. Now *that's* something to feel dirty about."

She tried to take his hand. "No, Jerram. I'm the one who should be apologizing. I really thought you were having the Nancy dreams and pretending you didn't. I felt betrayed."

"It's crazy, isn't it? We used to be on the same wavelength about everything; we knew exactly what we were both thinking. And now you're suspicious and I'm jealous."

"I know," she said. "I've felt bad about it." He was jealous not only of her dreams, but of Daniel, too. Would he be able to admit that?

"Nancy's put a wedge between us. I didn't even know her. What's she got against us?"

"It started before Nancy. I've been feeling apart from you for a long time. But maybe it's not a bad thing, maybe we just have to get on with our lives as individuals. Eventually we'll have to be more separate than we've been."

"Yes, professor," Jerram teased, a little more like himself. "But there has to be some reason why you get messages and I don't. We've always shared our dreams. All of a sudden, we don't. There must be a reason."

"Maybe only some people have this . . . gift. Maybe sharing our dreams wasn't the same as this. Some gift . . . I'm beginning to hate it. I do hate it."

"So I guess I should consider myself lucky," Jerram said. "But I wouldn't mind having it, too."

"You've got to tell Mackey for me. I don't know why Nancy told me about that skeleton first, but her friend's body is definitely in the caves."

Jerram nodded and looked toward the dark window. "At least I can do something to help," he said.

They found Cyn's body almost immediately. Silver got a lot of flack about that, people saying the police had been negligent in searching before. But Cyn hadn't been killed in the caves, and her body had only recently been put there.

"The lack of blood on the site tells us the murder took place elsewhere," the chief said. Rose wondered if that was why Nancy couldn't tell her sooner, because Cyn had been alive.

Rose knew she wouldn't feel the same about their annual Christmas pilgrimage to Ladyvale Farm. But before she even said anything, Dad came upstairs to her room and told her he'd found a great new nursery in Danville on the way home from work. "It was time for a change anyway, darlin'," he said. "That farm store was getting tacky."

"Thanks, Dad."

Silver Henning came to the house the next day, to talk to Rose. Mackey had not kept the fact that she was continuing to get psychic messages a secret. She remembered what he had said: "It's never wise to mask the truth."

Mom made Silver wait outside in the cold until she phoned Dad to find out if they needed a lawyer. Dad said it was enough if Mom stayed in the room, since Rose could hardly be under suspicion of murder, but they could always phone Diana Cambrick if anything got out of hand. Mom was resigned and tight-lipped, and curiously reluctant to ask Rose for more details about her sudden psychic powers. She seemed, more than ever, to be fervently wishing it would all go away. "Daddy said to cooperate," she told Rose. "Because we may need the police's help."

Rose was considered too weak to come downstairs, so Silver came up to her room, with his hat in his hands, looking tired and awkward. Detective O'Hara came in behind him, snappily dressed and decorated with jewelry, but even she looked subdued. There were only two chairs. Silver's bulk overflowed on the narrow desk chair.

Detective O'Hara took the comfortable armchair and regretted it. It was too casual and low and after a moment she shimmied forward and sat perched on the edge.

Mom stood next to the bed, and Rose could feel the tension in her body. She was ready to protect her daughter of course, but she seemed upset in some other way Rose didn't understand.

"We're ready to accept your . . . visions," Silver said with difficulty. "We know you were home, sick in bed, when the murder was committed."

Mom snorted. "You're not seriously suggesting my daughter needs an alibi?"

"I'm only suggesting that, hard as it is for a man of facts to accept, I've accepted that your daughter has some kind of clairvoyant powers."

"I don't know if that's accurate," Mom said. "I'm not sure that's the right term."

"Does it matter?" Detective O'Hara asked from her corner.

Mom turned to her. "Yes, it does. Because it's what will be spread all over the newspapers."

"We're doing our best to keep this quiet, Liz," Silver said.

"I'm sure you are." Mom seemed undecided. "I don't want Rose's name mentioned in connection with these murders."

"No one is mentioning her," O'Hara said.

"But it could come out, couldn't it? You've got to prevent that."

"We can try," Silver said soothingly. "Now, if we — "

Mom interrupted. "Your car is in my driveway for the second time in less than two weeks," she said to him, as if explaining things to a child. "And next door . . . next door lives the biggest gossip in Bethboro."

"Yes, well," Silver said edgily.

"So don't give me any of your sweet talk," Mom spat at him, surprising Rose.

"Nobody is going to think less of Rosecleer if they find out she's had some dreams."

Mom laughed bitterly. "I'm amazed," she said to him. "You don't get it, do you? Even though it's right in front of your nose. If the killer finds out about Rose, he'll come after her." She looked at Rose anxiously. "I wish you didn't have to hear that. But now that we're discussing this, we need to face facts." She turned back to Silver. "Rose could be in grave danger."

Silver shifted uneasily, and the desk chair gave out an ominous creak. O'Hara smoothed her skirt. There was something in their attitude that made Rose think they had already considered this possibility, but had put it aside in favor of finding out all they could, any way they could. And Rose had known it all along inside herself, from the time the car followed her that stormy night. She just hadn't wanted to admit it.

Silver Henning cleared his throat and got down to business.

"Rose, would you please tell us what circumstances led you to the knowledge of the body? Take it slowly, tell it in your own words."

Whose words would she tell it in?

"I don't really know that much," she said. Lamely, she added, "I just had this sort of dream and I heard the name Ladyvale Caves. That's it. Really. No big deal."

She wasn't going to tell them about what happened in the bathroom, or about Grace's swiveling head. O'Hara made a sound of protest, but Silver put up his hand. He leaned toward Rose, and she could see how tired he was.

"We need your help, Rose," he said gently. "Facts that have come to our attention suggest these three murders may not be the only ones. We need your help, whatever you can do for us, to find the other bodies, if there are any, God help us."

"Then let God help you," she said hoarsely. "I'm sick of finding dead people. I'm not doing it anymore."

Silver shrank back and Detective O'Hara looked shocked.

"You'd better go now." Mom's voice was stern, no nonsense. She hustled them out. Rose heard them go down the stairs, nobody speaking. There was the faraway sound of the front door shutting, and then footsteps coming back upstairs.

Mom stood silently in the doorway.

"Mom? Are you mad at me?"

"Oh, Rose, of course I'm not mad. What a silly thing to say."

"You seem mad sometimes. Is it because you're so worried that the killer might come for me?"

"Of course I'm worried about that."

"Something else, too?"

Mom sighed. "You're so different sometimes, I wonder how you got to be my daughter."

A warning pulsed in Rose's throat. "You mean because of this dream stuff?"

"I . . . no, no . . ." Mom turned away as if to get her bearings. "We've been through all that before, when you and Jerram were younger."

"But that wasn't like this, Mom, was it?"

Mom looked as if she would speak, as if something deep inside her wanted to get out, but then shook her head.

"Things from a long time ago. Nothing you need to worry about," she murmured abstractedly. Then added almost impatiently, "Just being a mother, that's all."

She gave Rose a pat and left the room. Rose felt totally bereft by that pat. It wasn't at all comforting. Instead she felt like a dog that had been patted, not human at all.

Fourteen

THEY NAMED HIM THE CHRISTMAS KILLER, BEcause of what looked like his trademark: leaving a red plastic poinsettia on his victims. That had been the incongruous flower on Nancy's pink jacket. One had been left with Cyn's body, too. Because of them, the police went back to the junkyard and found the remains of a similar, if dirtier, flower where the skeleton had been. They theorized that the skeleton girl had also been killed around Christmas.

His first letter arrived at the Bethboro newspaper office on Friday. It had a local postmark, which meant he was here, perhaps had always been here, not some stranger just passing through.

The envelope had been printed by hand in tiny letters and was sealed with a glob of red wax. There was an imprint stamped in the wax, but the police were keeping the exact design a secret, as they were certain facts they said made them certain the letter was authentic. Otherwise, the letter was reproduced intact, written meticulously in upper and lowercase block letters. A handwriting expert named Dipthorpe said the writer was someone who had a lot of patience and didn't mind slow, painstaking work. Did you need patience to kill someone? Rose would have imagined murder as swift and violent, a quicksilver act. It was horrible to think of his victims submitting to slow and painstaking work.

Dear Folks,

Only ten more shopping days until Christmas. I will be leaving you many more gifts besides the three you found and hope you will collect them all. Silent night, blood is bright, all is calm, blood is right. Think of me as the Christmas spirit. Death is sleepful peace. Peace is easeful death.

Happy Holiday Greetings from a friend.

"Oh, my God," Mom said when she read it. "This is the maniac who'll be after Rose."

"It could have been written by any nutter," Dad told her. "Don't jump to conclusions."

But Mom ignored him and pointed to another story on the same page. "This won't make things any better, either," she said.

The story mentioned a "local girl" who was helping the police. Although it didn't come right out and call her a psychic, linking her in the story with a bevy of famous psychics who'd helped the police made it fairly obvious that it was implied. Rose found it hard to read the piece all the way through. It gave her the creeps to be linked with people who sounded so peculiar.

"'Local girl' could mean anyone," Dad said.

Mom looked at him. "Everyone will know it's Rose, thanks to Barney."

"What does she know about it?"

"Silver's been up here twice," Mom said, sitting down hard on a kitchen chair. "She can put two and two together to make five. She always does."

"That biddy," Dad said coldly.

"To be fair, it may not be all Barney," Mom said. "Rose and Grace did go to the police the first time . . . any number of people might have started tongues wagging."

Grace, Rose thought. The killer could be after her, too. Rose longed to talk to her, to warn her, but had to be patient, since Grace would be in school. Rose was still home, on antibiotics, with Mom acting anxious and overprotective, not just because of germs.

"Don't worry before it's absolutely necessary," Dad said, finishing his coffee. "You girls sit tight and take it easy today." He'd delayed going into work, knowing Mom was upset. You girls. He sounded like Jerram. Or Jerram sounded like him.

The phone rang. It was Muriel, calling to see how Rose was. She hadn't been to class for a while.

"I'm not going to lose my solo, am I?" she asked.

"Of course not," Muriel said. "But will you be well enough in time for the recital?"

"I'm fine. Mom's just worried about me."

"That's what moms are for." Muriel chuckled.

Rose could talk to Muriel, she understood, she

was more in tune with the consciousness of the universe than parents would ever be. "Could I come down?" Rose asked impulsively. "Just to visit?"

A slight hesitation, then, "Of course, come over. Nothing's going on now, and it's only Leslie's baby tap class this afternoon; they're having a dress rehearsal to see if they can stay upright wearing their Uncle Sam hats. The new ones are heavier than last year's."

Mom didn't want Rose to go at all. Then said maybe, if she drove her down and back.

"Please, Mom, I've been cooped up in this house for a week. I need some exercise. And some . . . normality."

"We can't keep Rose a prisoner, even if you think it's for her own good," Dad said, putting on his coat. "I could drop her off on my way to the office, but she doesn't want that."

"What will people think," Mom insisted, "if they see her walking around town when she's supposed to be sick in bed?"

"I'll be taking a constitutional," Rose said. "Part of my recovery."

"Don't be so flippant," Mom bristled.

"I'm sorry, I wasn't — "

"Your mother's worried about the truant officer," Dad said lightly. He put his arm around Mom's shoulders.

"Well," she said, softening. "Don't be conspicuous, if you can help it."

"You do need to be careful, darlin'," Dad said.

"I promise I won't take any candy from strangers," Rose said, knowing it was the worst flippancy, but she couldn't help it.

"It's no longer a case of strangers, that's the trouble," Dad went on. His words hit home, making Rose realize just how upside down the world had become. You could start fearing the people you knew and trusted, people who'd always been around.

Mom made her bundle up, becoming distant and cool again, as if the only way she could deal with the strain was to withdraw into her private world. Rose didn't like this new Mom much. Mom had always been *Mom*, a secure person to count on, someone always there. My mother doesn't like me anymore, Rose thought irrationally. Mom doesn't like me getting messages from dead bodies. She wanted to talk about it. But how? *Hey, Mom, am I giving you the creeps? Are you scared of me?* How could you say things like that to your mother? Worse, how could you stand the answers?

For all her protestations of feeling fine, Rose found herself walking gingerly, like someone just released from the convalescent home. Like walking on eggs. The air was cold liquid going down her throat, and it shimmered in front of her eyes, turning everything into a slightly blurry photograph. This is my home, my town, this is Bethboro, she thought. This is where I have always felt safe. I refuse to believe that everyone is a potential killer. I refuse to believe in dark slimy secret places here.

No strange men in cars came by. The town seemed unusually quiet as if everyone might be home hiding under their beds.

She walked across the common toward Muriel's studio. Wallace Romola was sitting on a bench, hunched in his dirty overcoat and shawl, rocking himself and making little sounds, looking the picture of a town loony.

When he saw Rose, he got up and came forward in the crablike way he sometimes used, a sidewise shuffle. He seemed purposeful though, as if he wanted to say something.

Rose stopped. "Hello, Wallace."

"Mmmmm," he said and nodded rapidly a few times, his usual greeting.

He put out his hand automatically, palm upturned, but she didn't give him anything. It had become a sort of signal between them, a way for him to establish that she was still a girl he could respect. People gave Wallace money to make him go away, so they wouldn't be embarrassed by him, and he hated them for that.

"You going up there?" he asked in his gravelly voice and nodded toward Muriel's.

"Yes."

His eyes darted left and right, checking to see if anyone was in earshot. He leaned forward confidentially. Rose braced herself not to flinch. Wallace smelled sour, and his breath was always very bad.

"Nasty things going on."

"I know, Wallace."

"You keep watch up there."

"Where? At Muriel's?"

He nodded and ground his stained teeth together. His lips were chapped and cracked. Black and gray whiskers sprouted all over his chin and cheeks. But his eyes were beautiful: a clear, fragile blue that would have looked icy but for the long black eyelashes that shaded them.

"Why? Is she in trouble?"

"*You* take care," Wallace said. "It may be a trick of mirrors or it may be a miracle, I can't say. Persons in the dark look different than in the day. Bad persons might go inside there, or they might come out."

"I don't understand, Wallace. Are you saying someone is hanging around the dance school?"

"I tried to ask. She won't talk with me."

Rose recalled the night Muriel drove her home. She had been repulsed by Wallace.

"Are you sure about this?" Rose asked and noticed the hurt look in his eye. "I mean, is this something you should tell the police?"

Wallace looked uneasy. "No police," he said adamantly. The police had not been his favorite people even before they held him in connection with Nancy's murder. Periodically they grew disgusted with his vagrancy and forced him off the common.

"But if Muriel's in danger — "

"Maybe not her. Person been around many befores. Many many befores. Knows I watch here. Many dangers. I've suffered many bad hurts, many worries." Agitated, he danced from one foot to another, preparing to go off into one of his tirades. He often gave speeches from his bench on the common, and they were always about his grievances toward his family.

"Thank you, Wallace," she said gently and walked slowly away.

"Many bads, would I do that? No, but she never listened, she never paid attention to me," Wallace was saying. "Would I do that? Would I do that? No no no no."

Rose picked up speed in spite of not wanting to offend him. With talk like that, Wallace would get himself arrested. It gave her the shivers, hearing him denying he'd done bad things. But she was thoroughly disgusted with herself by the time she'd crossed the street and was at the door to the studio.

How could she be such a hypocrite? Wallace was innocent. He had no car, he didn't even know how to drive. Except. How did he total the Lamborghini? He must have taken driver's ed when he was in school, had a junior license. There were at least six cars in the big garage on the Romola estate. Who's to say he couldn't go up there and take one when he wanted to?

Wallace, she thought suddenly, could be one of those people with a split personality. What if part of him was good and wanted to warn her about the part of him that was bad? The part that hung around looking up at Muriel's windows, the part that might possibly do the bad things he was so busily denying right now?

No. She didn't believe it. Refused to believe it. She pushed open the door and walked up the flight of stairs to the studio.

Fifteen

MURIEL WAS TALKING ON THE PHONE IN HER office when Rose reached the top of the broad flight of wooden stairs. It must have been an important call because her hand was clenched on the receiver and she was hunched over in her chair, frowning.

"You can't keep doing this to me," she was saying. She looked up, saw Rose and swiveled her chair around. "Not now, she's here," Rose heard her say. When she hung up, her face was flushed.

"Sorry. I obviously interrupted. . . ."

"No, you didn't," Muriel said shortly, then brushed back her hair and seemed to relax. "You look so rosy!" She laughed. "Rosy Rose, did you walk? Want some hot tea?"

She chatted about the recital as she filled her electric kettle and plugged it in. She got herb tea bags from the desk drawer and took two earthenware mugs down from the bookshelf.

"You will be strong enough to dance in two weeks, won't you?" she asked.

"I've been sneak practicing in my bedroom. I wouldn't miss this chance for the world."

Muriel seemed distracted for a moment. The kettle began to whistle. She pulled the plug and poured steaming water over the tea bags. "I don't know how to say this, Rose. . . ."

"Say what?"

"The person I told you might come from New York . . ."

Rose's heart sank. "He's not coming. I knew it was too good to be true."

"I'm sorry." Muriel handed her a mug of hot tea. "It's disappointing but it isn't the end of the world."

"Right."

"It's my fault. I shouldn't have got your hopes up."

"What happened, anyway?"

"Oh . . . he's very busy." She waved her hand airily. "He has a lot of commitments."

Rose sipped her tea in silence. She'd known Muriel five years. She'd grown up studying with Muriel, she wasn't ten years old anymore. Muriel was covering up her feelings. Rose only hoped that the guy had really canceled, and that it wasn't because Muriel had decided she wasn't good enough for him to see and had told him not to come. She felt too gutless to ask directly. She didn't want to hear that kind of truth.

"Doesn't matter," she said, trying to rise above it.

"You'll have other opportunities."

"It's in the hands of the gods. Isn't that what you always say?"

Muriel smiled. "Call it fate, Rose. But yes, I do believe that some things are just out of our hands. Perhaps there's a good reason for this now, but you may not see the reason for a long time to come."

"Like I'm not exactly star quality?"

"Nothing like that — you know you're a good dancer. Try to see it as positive. This man might not be the right person in your life now. Maybe your karmas don't match!" Muriel laughed lightly. She seemed almost relieved, making Rose wonder anew what had really happened between the two of them. Rose took another sip of tea and felt lonely. "I came down here because I couldn't stand it at home."

"It's getting to you, isn't it? That inflammatory article in the paper. . . . the editor should be shot."

"He's only doing his duty, I suppose. People have a right to know the killer sent a letter," Rose said, sounding like Mr. Keller the history teacher.

"I'm not so sure. But that's not what I'm talking about. I mean the other stuff about you being a psychic. That's an invasion of privacy."

"You think they were writing about me?"

Muriel looked uncomfortable. "Your name wasn't mentioned, but you know what this town's like."

It was just as Mom had predicted. "People spread rumors, but it doesn't mean they're true," Rose retorted, feeling offended.

Muriel looked at her over the rim of her mug. "*Mea culpa*. I'm getting more like this one-horse town every day."

Rose had never seen Muriel so jittery before. Usually she was solid as a rock, always ready to calm everybody else down. But maybe it was the recital. Muriel was always nervous at Christmastime, as preparations for the recital came to a head. Still, it was rubbing off on Rose. The visit was not turning out to be a success.

Muriel was suddenly brisk. "So, you don't have any of these famous powers after all. What a shame. You could have told me how the baby tap class would do. According to the paper, a psychic can predict almost anything."

"Like what?" Rose asked.

"Haven't you read it? Wait, I have it here." She rummaged through the papers and magazines on her desk and pulled it out.

Rose read more thoroughly this time, realizing the implications. The psychics in the story had not only located bodies or missing people but had predicted plane crashes and earthquakes, the collapse of bridges and all kinds of disasters. And they had a good track record. She threw the paper aside angrily.

"I can't do all that."

"Thank goodness," Muriel said. "But can you do *any* of it?" she added, in a quiet voice.

"The truth is I don't *do* anything. I've had a couple of weird dreams, that's all."

"Dreams that told you where to find these girls?"

"Sort of like that."

"And nothing else? You can't read minds. You don't know who the killer is?"

"I already said no. You're not going to start

being afraid of me, are you?" The thought of it made her uneasy. She turned it into a joke. "I didn't scare the New York guy off, did I?"

But Muriel didn't laugh. She took the empty mugs and put the kettle back on. "It must be difficult, but at least you have your family. You're lucky."

"I guess so."

"Families are important. Don't undervalue them, Rose." She fussed with the tea things. "I don't have a family myself . . . not really. It's . . . not good to be all alone in the world."

"I didn't realize . . . I guess I sounded flippant. My mother always tells me I am."

"Around the holidays is when you miss having a family most," Muriel mused.

"But you must have had one once. Didn't you?" Rose hoped she wasn't overstepping the bounds.

"Our . . . my parents are dead. I don't have very many good memories. Christmas was . . . not a happy time for me." Muriel's voice trailed off. Then she said, "But you must have wonderful holidays with your family."

"Christmas is usually our best time. This year seems to be going a little weird, though, with these murders. Dad's just Dad, but Mom's acting more hyper every day. And Jerram . . . well, he's . . . Jerram."

"You're very close to your brother, aren't you?"

Rose nodded. Unaccountably, tears welled up. "At least we *were* close."

"Not anymore?"

"We seem to be growing apart. I can't really explain it."

"He feels like a stranger sometimes? Not like the brother you had before?"

"That's exactly it." Rose was amazed at her insight. Foolishly, the tears spilled over.

"Rose, you're crying, I'm sorry. . . ."

She wiped them away impatiently. "It's nothing."

Muriel came to sit down next to her, bringing wafts of her familiar spicy perfume. "No, it *is* painful," she said. "And you need to experience the pain. Because that's the only way it will ever go away."

She squeezed Rose's hand, and Rose squeezed back. "Thanks," she said, looking up. She was astonished to see that Muriel was crying, too.

"Holidays," Muriel said, trying to smile. "They make you happy and sad at the same time."

Sixteen

WHEN SHE LEFT MURIEL, THE SKY WAS DEEPENING from blue to purple, and the lingering winter light seemed surreal. Rose didn't see Wallace as she went back across the common. She didn't mind walking home in the nearly dark but she worried about not telling Muriel what Wallace had said. The visit had ended so strangely, with Muriel apologizing for crying and Rose feeling embarrassed and curious but not wanting to pry. But then, what danger would she have warned her about? Wallace often did just talk nonsense.

Lost in thought, her pace slowed. A car pulled up beside her, and the driver's voice gave her a start.

"I'm looking for the Danville Road."

A man in a business suit and tie leaned toward the passenger window. He seemed vaguely familiar to Rose, but she couldn't get a really good look at his face in the fading afternoon light.

"Danville Road? You mean route 7?"

"That's the one."

She had to think. "Go up three streets, take a

right on Franklin. Then down a few blocks to North Beacon — "

"Hold it, this sounds complicated," he said, laughing. "A right on Franklin. Is there a sign?"

"I'm not sure. Some roads aren't marked."

He looked at his watch and frowned. "Just my luck when I'm in a hurry."

"Well, if you find North Beacon you'll come right to route 7."

"Thanks," he said. "Say, you wouldn't want to hop in and show me where Franklin is, would you?"

It wasn't until that moment that she realized her stupidity. She backed away from the car.

The street was lonely, with houses set back behind tall hedges. There was no one in sight, little traffic. Rose looked around in panic.

"Now, take it easy," the man said. "Don't worry. I'm glad to see you being cautious. Sorry I scared you, Rose."

She was surprised. "You know me?"

"Rose Potter? I'm acquainted with your dad. Hey, I'm in a real rush; the wife's not well." He put the car in gear. "Guess I can find this Franklin Street. . . ." He left the words hanging and looked hopeful. Now that he was ready to drive off, she felt safer. And a little sorry for him. It would only take a moment to show him Franklin Street. She noticed he had opened the passenger side door.

"Yo, Rose!" a voice called out.

Daniel was loping up the street toward her. Her heart hesitated oddly, then thumped to make up for the missed beat. Daniel looks beautiful, she thought, and forgot the car. She jumped as it pulled off with a roar.

"Who was that?" Daniel asked.

"Guy wanting directions."

Daniel shook his head. "You know better than that, Rose," he said with concern.

"What? Oh, there's nothing to worry about. He knows my dad."

"I'm glad to hear it. What are you doing wandering around in the dark, anyway?"

The sun was just a small bright chink between the trees. "There's no curfew, is there?"

"Should be."

"If you're so worried, why not walk me home?" Rose blurted out before she lost her nerve.

But he was already leading her along in a protective way.

"So what are you doing up here?" she asked.

"Looking for you."

"Come on."

He put up his hands. "Truth. I phoned and your mother said you were at Muriel's. I went to Muriel's and she said you were walking home. So here I am. And lucky thing, too, or you might have been abducted."

"I *told* you, he knew me. Really, Daniel, what will happen if we start suspecting everybody?"

"Not everybody. Just strangers in dark blue Shadows."

"I didn't know you were so poetic."

"The car that guy was driving . . . blue Dodge Shadow."

"Oh." It seemed so typical that a male would know the make of a car. Maybe he even had memorized the license plate while she'd acted the female airhead, eager to be helpful, oblivious of danger, just ripe for being saved by a knight in shining armor. Well, she didn't mind if the knight was Daniel.

"I never got your message when I was sick. My brother forgot."

"Wasn't anything important."

"Bet you wanted to give me Keller's history assignment."

"I phoned because I wanted to talk to you."

"About what?"

He stopped walking. "Because I missed you."

She could feel a wisecrack ready to pop out of her mouth. As if she needed to make fun of his honesty, to make herself feel less creepy. She'd learned that from Jerram: cover up feelings by acting contemptuous or bored. Well, now it was time to unlearn. She took a deep breath and tried to do what Muriel was always saying to do: get in touch with the real feelings inside. Get in touch and don't be ashamed to reveal them.

"I . . . missed you, too, Daniel."

He looked into her eyes, and she forced herself not to turn away.

"Good," he said. "That's settled." He leaned over to kiss her.

It was a right kiss, a feeling kiss even though they were hardly touching, even though their lips were cold. It was soft and tender. It was the kind of kiss she'd always dreamed of.

She melted toward it, into it, would have lost herself in it, but there was a sudden sound, a susurrus of wings, a sad keening wind that brushed past like the hurried but insistent touch of frigid fingers. It drew them apart. They both had felt it. Daniel looked up and down the street that was suddenly dark and empty except for the red taillights of a distant car winking around a bend.

They put their arms around each other and walked on toward Rose's house.

Speaking would have broken the moment. But there were things that had to be said. Things like seeing each other again, and spending time together. And finally, things to be said about what had just happened.

"It was like something evil had been watching us," Daniel said.

"I know, I felt it. But it seems so . . ."

"Unbelievable?"

"Yes. Silly."

"Murder is evil, not silly." His fingers, warm now, traced the outline of her face, lingered at her lips. Then he grew practical. "You have a way with you, Rosecleer. Trust your instincts . . . or whatever they're called. Trust yourself."

"But you felt something, too," Rose said, eager for him to acknowledge that such "gifts" were not hers alone.

He shook his head. "I felt it through you."

She drew away, but he pulled her back and hugged her.

After a moment he whispered in her ear: "Your mother's watching. Otherwise I'd kiss you. A real kiss this time."

"Wasn't the kiss you gave me real?"

"Just you wait and see."

"I'd better go in now."

"I'll call you tomorrow," he said. In full view of Mom staring out the window, he gave her lips a puritan peck.

" 'Bye, Daniel," she called, long after he couldn't hear, just for the chance of saying his name.

When Grace phoned on Saturday to report on her date with Gregory, Rose was capable of only half listening. The date had been a disaster.

"He didn't talk, Rose," Grace shrieked in despair. "I mean it, I'm not exaggerating. He said exactly eight — count 'em — eight words all night."

"Oh, Grace, how terrible." Rose thought of Daniel and talking with him for almost an hour on the telephone Friday night, and another hour that morning.

"Want to know what they were?"

"Hmmmm?"

"Rose, are you listening? He said 'Hi' when he saw me and he said 'to the movies' when I asked him where we were going. Then he asked 'Want popcorn?' and after the movie he said it was 'okay' and then ' 'bye.' That's exactly eight words. Eight words in four hours. And he didn't even take me out afterwards. We passed Lucky's, and everybody was in there having pizza. But I was actually glad we didn't go in because I would have been mortified to be seen with him."

"Yeah," Rose said.

"Why do I get the feeling you're not concentrating?"

"I am, I am . . ."

"No, you're not. You're . . . wait a minute Rose, hang on a sec."

Grace's mother said something about wanting to use the phone.

"All right, all right, I said okay," Grace yelled to her mother. "I gotta go now," she said to Rose. "I'll call back later."

Grace didn't call back, but Rose wasn't thinking about it anyway. As Grace had said, she wasn't concentrating. She was thinking about Daniel, feeling alternately over the moon and down in the dumps. Happy one minute, confused the next. She was overwhelmed with a new truth: Nothing was as interesting or as important as Daniel.

She spent most of the early afternoon lying in bed, staring at the ceiling. Every once in a while she'd think about getting up and doing something productive and then just keep on lying there. But then she was only doing what Muriel advised, sitting in it like Buddha.

Eventually, the voices from below intruded: Barney and her parents talking excitedly. With great effort, she shifted her mind off Daniel. Maybe tuna on toasted rye. Amazingly, she was hungry. She'd always thought you lost your appetite when you were in love.

Jerram burst into the room, destroying mouth-watering visions.

"Did you hear?" he said.

"Hear what?"

"No, of course you didn't hear."

She struggled to a half-sitting position. "Jerram, what are you talking about?"

"Fast-breaking news from the Barney network. They've identified the skeleton you found. And another girl is missing."

She sat all the way up. "The skeleton *I* found?"

"You know what I mean, Rose. It's a girl from Danville, Helena Klout, missing for five years. Her family was convinced she'd run away. They'd had a big fight about her seeing some guy, and she'd left a note."

"So the boyfriend probably did it."

"No, he never left. Has an alibi, checked out even after all this time. She wrote to him, too, saying she was going to the city. She never got there, obviously. It all fits in. Her parents said she always hitched rides. Whoever this guy is, he's using a car, getting his victims to take a ride with him."

She lay back down. "I really don't care anymore."

"You have to care," Jerram cried.

"No, I don't."

Jerram was agitated. "But this new girl, you have to help find her."

"She'll only be dead," Rose said and saw Jerram flinch. "I told the police, I don't want to keep finding dead bodies."

"But you might get a message anyway, whether you want to or not. You'd tell then, wouldn't you?"

She gave him a defiant glare. "I don't know! You think it's so easy? Well, why don't you take a nap and get a message and see how *you* like it. As far as I'm concerned, I'm out to lunch."

"I never saw you like this, Rose," Jerram said. "I can't believe it."

She turned away, afraid to see that Jerram was near to tears.

"Please?" he said. And when she didn't answer, he quietly left the room.

Jerram suddenly gone altruistic? The gruesome Jerram? What got into him all of a sudden?

She refused to feel bad about it and shut her ears to her brother's accusations. He had no right to accuse her. He didn't know what it was like.

Daniel, she thought. I really need to talk to you now. Only how can I possibly explain all this? You said I should trust myself. But I don't know what to do. Am I obligated to keep getting messages? Must I go on talking to the dead? I'd rather forget it and stick with the living. Like you.

Part Five

Him

SHE IS A STRONG ONE. CLEVER. BUT I AM LEARNING her ways. The newspapers hint about powers but I don't believe she can match me. It will be nice to play with her for a while.

They must all look into my face and see my real self. Then death will bring them the flower bloom of love.

Tomorrow I have much to do. I will prepare the little gift with red blood ribbons and leave it for them. I have taken the risk again but everything is all right. Wollenschaft is gone, and the house is quiet and empty. No one to spy on me.

After the gift is delivered, I think I will buy myself a Christmas tree.

I am in such a good mood. How does that old song go? Oh, what a beautiful Christmas. Everything's going my way. But perhaps best not to think of old songs, old anything. Reminds me of the mothertimes. Mothertimes, othertimes, bad times, death times.

Rose

Seventeen

THE CHURCH WAS PACKED ON SUNDAY. DAD said, "We should have bought reserved seats."

Mom said, "Sssssh, Carl," so loud everyone in the last few pews turned around. They slipped into seats near the back, and Mom's face was bright red.

"The Emersons and the Merleys are down in front," she observed in a whisper. "I wonder if Reverend Fairley is going to say something special."

"The whole town's running scared," Jerram said.

He was right. The church was filled with a need that was almost tangible . . . you could feel it pulsating with the music of the organ. It seemed frighteningly wrong, as if the adults of Bethboro had become little children again.

Rose felt scruffy and tired and hadn't wanted to come to church. Saturday had been horrible. It seemed like everybody had wanted something from her. Jerram had gone off in a sulk after trying to make her feel guilty, as if she was shirking her duty by not going to sleep on the spot to get a dream message from Nancy. Right after, Chief Henning had phoned to ask if he could question Rose about the same thing. Luckily, Dad had said no. He told Silver they'd have to consult their lawyer, Ms. Cambrick, before Rose could be involved.

After a depressing supper, she had an overwhelming need to talk, to sort it all out. Jerram had always been the one she could talk to, and now she couldn't.

She'd phoned Grace but her mother said she was out.

"Tell her to call me," Rose said, then impulsively she dialed Daniel's number and asked him to come over. He said yes. No questions, no explanations, he just said yes.

When he arrived, face red-bitten from the cold because he'd walked all the way, Rose knew she wanted to tell him everything. And yet, in spite of the trust she felt for him, she kept holding back. Allegiance to Jerram kept getting in the way. It was as if she would be betraying him by talking so intimately to someone else. But she forced it out, half expecting Daniel to feel repulsed. He took her hand instead, and held it firm as she talked.

"Do you think I'm wrong not to help the police?" Rose asked Daniel.

There was a long pause before Daniel answered. "It would be easy to say yes. But it's always easy to do the right thing when you yourself don't have to do it. I don't know, Rose. *Can* you help them?"

Rose was startled. She hadn't considered that and neither had Silver Henning. They had all begun to assume she could make contact with Nancy at will.

"That helps more than anything anybody has said," she told Daniel. "I'm not the one who has the power. It's Nancy. It's really up to her."

"And if you do get another message from her?"

"I'd like to wash my hands of the whole thing. But I guess you know the answer. If Nancy decides to tell me where this new body is, what else can I do but let Silver know? Although . . . it all seems so pointless when they're dead already."

"But maybe the faster they find the victims, the closer they'll get to knowing the killer."

"I never realized how practical you can be," Rose said, smiling.

"Lots of things you don't know about me," he said.

"And maybe things you don't know about me, either," she said sadly. "You don't think I'm some kind of freak, do you?"

"No, of course not, you know that."

"Then what? What am I?"

"You'll find out, Rose. Look on the good side. It could be a wonderful thing."

He kissed her outside in the cold, out of Mom's sight. Rose went to her room without seeing Jerram. His closed door was like an accusation. She slept fitfully during the night, aware of every time she turned over. Nancy had not appeared. There had been no messages.

But when she woke up on Sunday morning, her head ached, as if something had been trying to get inside it, as if she had spent the entire night forcibly keeping it out.

The service was about to start. As the Reverend Joan Fairley walked to the altar, and the congregation rose, Daniel's words came back to her. "You'll find out," he'd said. Find out what she really was.

It was odd as they went through the service to hear so many voices responding, singing the hymns with such strength. Usually the organ drowned everybody out, but now the joined voices were loud, and even the draggiest hymns sounded better than they ever had before.

Rose had never really liked this new church. Everybody was very proud when it was built, but she preferred the old church, cramped and dark with creaking floors and smelling of incense, an atmosphere suited to meditation and prayer. This bright new church, with its long uncolored windows, seemed too efficient and businesslike for rituals. But now as she watched the sunlight falling in bright shafts from the tall windows, she could understand why everybody had come.

The sermon reminded them to trust God's will, to stand against evil. And the prayer afterwards was for the grief of the Emersons and Merleys and the Klouts in Danville, and the parents of the victim that had yet to be found, a girl named Carla Fentesso, from a nearby town. The Reverend Joan asked God to give the town courage and strength to stand together. The

Amen that followed sounded more like the cry of a tent revival meeting than the congregation of their sedate church.

The organ struck up the recessional, and people began to straggle out into the aisle. It was polite to let those in front go first, so Nancy's and Cyn's parents were the first to come up.

Mrs. Emerson stopped abruptly when she reached their pew. Behind her, her husband and the Merleys stopped short.

Mom smiled sympathetically, but Mrs. Emerson's face twisted in anger. She lifted a black-gloved hand and pointed.

"You!" she said in a voice loud enough to carry over the organ's muted music. Rose heard her mother's sharp intake of breath and murmur of surprise. Someone gripped Rose's arm from behind, either Dad or Jerram.

"Witch!" Mrs. Emerson screamed. The organ stopped. People stopped. Everything stopped. "We don't want your kind here."

Her husband was saying something ineffectual, like "now, now" but he didn't stop her. Mrs. Merley tried to interrupt. She looked weary and distressed, her eyes red-rimmed. "It's just that we don't like your predictions," she said. "We don't want any more killings."

"It's not my fault," Rose tried to say. Her throat was dry. "I didn't make anything happen."

There was a rumble among the congregation as Mr. Emerson dragged his wife away. The Merleys looked sorry but went along, avoiding Rose's eyes. She felt numb and something was wrong in her chest. It was hard to breathe. Mrs.

Emerson's accusation still rang in her ears. And she could hear other voices, too, like the buzzing of insects. "What's she got to do with it?" "They say she knows things." "It sounds unnatural."

Someone was trying to get Rose to move. She realized one of the church wardens had come up through the crowded aisle. "Please, please," he said soothingly. "Come this way, come this way," and he gently urged the crowd back and escorted Rose and her family up the side aisle and out the vestry door.

"So sorry. She's terribly upset," he said.

"Of course she's upset, my poor child!" Mom cried before realizing he had been apologizing for Mrs. Emerson. Dad put his arm around Mom. Rose's hand was gripped hard in Jerram's. He said nothing, just pulled her toward the parking lot and their car.

"How could she?" Mom kept asking as they got in.

"You don't want to pay any attention," Dad said as he maneuvered the car into the road. "Grief does strange things to people."

"There's no excuse for a thing like that," Mom replied. "No excuse at all. And in a church!"

Tituba, Sarah Osburne, Sarah Good, I know now how you felt, you first three accused witches of Salem, Rose thought. I am going to my own home but it might just as well be to Ipswich Prison with you. I'd been so complacent when I gave my report in Mr. Keller's class, hadn't I? Looking at it all like some smarmy psychiatrist. Simple case of mass hysteria, all paranoid delusions. What had I known about it? Absolutely nothing at all.

Eighteen

AFTER CHURCH THEY ALWAYS WENT TO CUSHman's, a restaurant that was a town institution. Mom and Dad went there as kids and so did their parents before them. The decor never changed, just became a little more worn and stained. There were brass sconces on the walls, oversized padded booths and tables set with pink linen cloths and napkins. A crew of ancient waitresses wearing pink dresses and frilly caps and aprons rushed around. The atmosphere was one of refined homeliness, with subdued voices and the gentle clatter of plates, and an unforgettable aroma of apple pie and strong-brewed coffee. Everybody went to Cushman's for Sunday dinner after church.

Today, Dad headed the car right for the restaurant. It took Mom a moment to notice and then she said, "Oh, no, Carl, we aren't going in there!"

"Don't see why not," he said, his jaw set.

"You can't be serious," Mom protested. "Not after all that."

"I don't think we should take *that* seriously, Liz. We have to act normal, do what we always do. Otherwise, this could escalate."

"Dad's right," Jerram said. But Rose agreed with Mom. She had no desire to eat a Cushman's Sunday Special. The thought of prime rib of beef with roasted whites or honey-baked ham with mashed sweets made her gag.

"I'm not going in," she said as they pulled into the parking lot.

"Now, Rose," Dad began. But there, going through the glass doors of the restaurant, were the Emersons and the Merleys. "Then again, maybe not."

There was dead silence in the car as they got back on the road. Then Dad broke in with a voice determined to be jolly. "We're not going to let this get to us, are we, troops?"

Nobody answered.

"Come on, come on. Are we going to take this lying down?"

Mom gave a weak laugh. "No, Carl, of course not."

"I say we go get our Christmas tree right now," Dad suggested. "Then we bring it home and set it up and spend the afternoon decorating."

"But . . ." Mom began. The family tradition was to save the tree trimming until Christmas eve.

"And order in a pizza," Dad said.

"Only if it's pepperoni and mushroom," Jerram said.

"Not pepperoni," Mom protested. "Sausage, okay, but no pepperoni."

"Sausage, mushroom and green peppers," Jerram compromised.

Dad noticed Rose wasn't talking. "What's your choice, darlin'?"

"Sausage, mushroom, green peppers and anchovies." She tried to get in the mood.

"Good girl," Dad said.

As he had promised, they went for the tree at the new nursery in Danville instead of Ladyvale Farm. The trees were more expensive than at the farm, but Dad paid for the Scotch pine without a murmur. And keeping with tradition, he suggested Jerram and Rose go into the Christmas Shop for a new ornament while he and Mom looked at the wreaths. They were all trying hard to play their parts and not doing too badly.

"You want me to pick?" Jerram asked, and Rose realized she'd been staring at the ornaments tied to a sprayed silver display tree.

"Lots of angels this year," she said. "None of them look like Nancy."

"Come on, Rose. I'm sorry for the way I acted yesterday."

"You're only saying that because you're afraid I'll put a hex on you."

"Just forget what Mrs. Emerson said."

"You really do think I should try to get in touch with Nancy, don't you?"

He was silent a moment. "Yes and no."

"What does that mean?"

"Ambivalence, that's what. Yes, I think you should use whatever power you have. No, I don't think you need to put yourself through hell because it won't matter, this new girl will be dead when they find her." He said this bitterly and turned away, flicking at the ornaments roughly.

A salesclerk came over. "Can I help you two kids with something?"

Jerram gave him a look. "We two kids want one of your angels."

"Right you are! Take your pick."

Jerram looked at Rose, and she said, "Any one will do," losing what little enthusiasm she'd had.

He peered closely into the squinched angel faces. "This one's got too much lipstick on. This one looks drunk. Here's one with the face of innocence."

The clerk laughed nervously and took the angel away to be rung up and bagged.

"I have to explain," Jerram said while they waited to pay. "I've been a turd."

Rose choked down a laugh when she saw he was deadly serious about something.

"Okay. I'll listen."

He held the door as they left the shop. "Not now."

"Well, that was nice," Mom said as they got into the car.

"A little Christmas spirit does wonders," Dad said, turning the key in the ignition. He backed the car carefully out of the parking slot while Mom kept her hand out the window, clutching at the tree on top just to make sure. Down at the end of the parking lot, a man in a suit was hoisting a tree onto the top of a blue car.

"Oh, hey," Rose said, sitting forward to get a better look.

"What is it, Rose?" Mom asked worriedly. "Is the tree okay?"

"Yes, sure. Is that guy a friend of yours, Dad?"

"What guy?" Dad asked, his attention on maneuvering the car.

"In that blue car over there."

Dad took a look, then changed gears and turned his eyes on the road. "Can't really see from here."

"Watch it, Carl, there's traffic," Mom warned as he pulled out onto the highway.

"What was that stuff about a man in a car?" Jerram asked when they were home, waiting for the pizza and for Dad to find the Christmas tree stand he'd so carefully stowed somewhere in the attic.

"I think it was the same guy who stopped to ask directions. But what were you going to explain to me?"

Jerram ignored her question. "When did he ask for directions? Today?"

"No." With a resigned sigh, she told him about it.

"Let me get this straight. A strange man stops you and you talk to him?"

"I'm not stupid. I didn't get in the car."

"Ever hear of brute force? Don't assume these girls are getting into cars on their own free will. Maybe Helena Klout did, to hitch a ride to New York, but we don't know about Nancy or Cyn. Carla Fentesso certainly didn't."

"How do you know what she did? Anyway, I

wasn't in any danger. Daniel came along."

"That explains everything." He stuck his headphones on his ears. Rose pulled them off.

"Everything's a mess, Jerram," she shouted. "Nothing is like it used to be between us. It can't be. You've got to stop being jealous of Daniel."

Jerram shifted uncomfortably.

"I'm not jealous. Why should I be jealous? We're brother and sister, for God's sake."

"I didn't mean it that way," she said, feeling crawly. "I mean you haven't got anybody. We used to be all we needed, the two of us. Now . . . it's going to keep getting different."

"I'm worried about you, that's all. Brotherly worry. I never thought of you as a ditz, but here you are giving directions to strangers. Didn't you think of the danger?"

"I did and I didn't," she said, remembering the night she went up to Mackey's. Maybe she should have reported it all to the police. She might have, if she hadn't been so busy reporting all the other stuff. Somehow her own safety had been lost in the shuffle.

Jerram threw up his hands in a dramatic way, then crashed into a chair and slouched glumly. "I give up."

"You're right, of course. I should have been suspicious. I mean, if he knows Dad he must come from around here. How come he can't find his way to route 7?"

"That's what I mean, Rose. You can't dismiss it."

"But he looked familiar and ordinary. Not the way you'd think a murderer would look."

"There is no way a murderer looks. I've been doing some research. Ever hear of Son of Sam?"

"Who's he?"

"Mass murderer in the 1970s. Innocent face, baby-blue eyes. Shot girls in their cars. Cars and murderers seem to go together. Neighbors said he looked like a nice boy."

"Why are you reading books about mass murderers? There's enough in the local paper."

"I want to know how their minds work. Then maybe I — "

The doorbell rang.

"The pizza man cometh," Jerram said.

But it was the Reverend Joan Fairley, come to talk about what happened in church. She said a lot of the same things Rose said in her report on the Salem witches. When people were frightened and upset, they looked for something or someone to blame.

Mom nodded along with the words, but Dad frowned.

"That's all well and good, but this is the twentieth century, and Mrs. Emerson is an intelligent woman. There's no excuse for what she said to Rosecleer. She's responsible, and she's the one who should be up here apologizing."

"I understand how you feel," Joan Fairley said.

"With all due respect, no, I don't think you know how I feel. My daughter was made a fool of in front of half the town. Are we supposed to just forgive and forget?"

"Carl," Mom cautioned, but he was not to be stopped.

"There's a limit," he said. "What happens to

the multitudes may be God's design, but what happens to my daughter is my business."

Joan Fairley stood up. "My concerns are with the soul, Mr. Potter. If I can be of any help or comfort to you in that capacity, please let me know."

"Thanks for coming by," Mom said, seeing her to the door. The pizza man was standing there, ready to knock. Mom juggled shaking the Reverend Joan's hand and paying for the pizza. She came back into the living room, bringing an aroma of sausage and anchovies and a whiff of the cold outdoors.

"Really, Carl," she said, standing in the living room doorway, balancing the pizza box in her arms.

But Dad stood his ground. "One thing you need to learn is to be responsible for what you say in this world. Be willing to back it up, stand up for it, stand by it. I don't think Mrs. Emerson is prepared to do that."

"Of course she won't stand by it, not in this day and age," Mom said. "Nobody believes in witches anymore."

"Superstition is a powerful force," Dad said. The way he said it made Rose feel very still for a moment.

Then Mom announced, "Let's eat this thing before it gets cold."

Pizza is good for the soul, Rose thought, as she bit into her second slice. It made you feel normal. Witches and dead bodies didn't seem real when you were eating a sausage and anchovy pizza and slugging it down with Coke. She kept one eye on the number of slices Jerram was consuming, keeping a fair count, and she felt better than she had since the morning.

They had all relaxed by the time the box was empty and the table was a wreck of crumbs, ends and empty glasses. They went back into the living room to work on the tree, feeling more like a family than they had in days, Rose thought. Mom's face had softened, the worried lines had faded away.

When the phone rang later, Dad answered. "For you, Rose," he said, and she hoped it was Daniel.

"Heard there was a wee spot of trouble at church today," Old Mackey's voice said. "Are you all right?"

"Sure, I guess so," Rose replied.

"I don't like to be the voice of doom, but this kind of thing could continue," Mackey said. "Forewarned is forearmed. It may help you to get to know yourself, Rose, the better to stand up to such antics. You must face your enemy."

"What enemy?" Rose asked.

"Ah, but don't you already know that?" Mackey said.

When Rose didn't answer, he added softly. "When you want the help, it's waiting in the form of my sister, Miss Mackey. She knows more about this sort of thing than I do. She can guide you through these dangerous waters. Consider it, Rose."

The enemy? Rose thought when she'd hung up. Was Mackey telling her it was herself?

Nineteen

When Rose went up to get ready for bed, Nancy was staring into her bedroom window. White face, eyes like black coals, Nancy had changed. No more piglet roundness. Her face was angular, the cheeks sunken, the skin taut. It was easy to see the skull beneath the skin.

Rose stared back at her, heart thundering. A bawling howl started deep inside her throat.

This was not as easy as a dream. This was a waking nightmare. She ran to the window and pulled the curtains shut.

She shoved a tape into her player and turned up the volume. Nancy's voice broke into the room and shook her by the shoulders.

"Listen to me, Rose," it said. "Like you did before."

"I'm listening," Rose said weakly. This is what Chief Henning and Jerram wanted her to do. This is what Mrs. Emerson didn't want. Mom called up the stairs, "Will someone please turn that music down?"

"It's hard for me, Rose," Nancy said.

"Hard for you! What about me?" Rose cried.

"Shut up and listen, Rose."

"I'll listen if you tell me something decent once in a while. You're always too late, Nancy! Why don't you tell me before they're killed? Why don't you get off your dead ass and tell me who did it!"

There was no answer from Nancy. Rose ran to the window and tore the curtains open again. Nancy's eyes burned into her own. Then Mom burst into the room and there was a flicker, like a candle snuffed out, and Nancy was gone.

"Rose! That music!"

"Sorry." She turned the player off.

"And why aren't you in bed? Come on, shake a leg."

"Mom? Did you ever notice that I was different?"

Mom laughed. "You and your brother were always a little different. But that's no excuse for blasting the house down at midnight."

"I'm serious. Could we talk about it, please? What about when I was born? Did anything happen?"

"Only that you came into the world yelling your head off."

"I mean something . . . like anything . . . well, something you couldn't explain."

"I don't know what you're on about. Your birth was perfectly normal, Rose. Remember what your father said and don't let Mrs. Emerson get to you. All right. You seem to have some kind of sixth sense. But that's not so strange. Lots of people have premonitions; maybe you're just better at them. I don't want you going around thinking you're some kind of oddity, and I don't want you getting a big head. The best thing to do is try to forget about it." She went over to draw the curtains back across the window.

"That's just great, Mom. Forget about it?"

"We're not going to let this wreck our lives."

"Like it's my fault? I didn't decide to do this, you know. It just happened to me. That's why I asked you, what's different about me? And you just tell me to forget it."

"You're tired, dear," Mom said. Her face was expressionless as she gave Rose a peck of a kiss good night. "Have a good sleep. Things will look brighter in the morning."

Rose was tired but didn't think she was going to sleep much.

Please, please, she prayed. Please don't let her come back again tonight.

The man was hoisting something onto the top of his blue car, tying it down. Rose tried to blink away the cobwebs in front of her eyes. It was not a Christmas tree, it was a body. The head lolled, and the limbs kept slipping off. He tossed them around like dead fish and secured them with a hairy rope. The lardy flesh cracked and split as he pulled the rope tighter. Little worms came crawling out. He laughed like a raucous mynah bird. "Can you tell me the way to Danville dump?" he shouted.

She woke as the watery light of dawn was seeping around the tightly closed curtains. Just a regular nightmare, not a Nancymare.

But her mind was racing. Should she tell Silver about the blue car? But what if the man was innocent?

Anyway, he had been buying a Christmas tree. Would a murderer buy a tree? And he knew her name. The killer couldn't know that. Even if he'd read the newspaper; it only said "local girl." There was no mention of her name, no photograph.

She couldn't go around making accusations; it would make everything worse if she was wrong. Nobody would believe her about anything after that. The only good thing she could do was to name the killer when she was absolutely sure.

Unable to go back to sleep, Rose got up and went downstairs into her father's den. On the bookshelf were the family photo albums, a continuing history of the Potter family. Rose pulled out the albums and brushed them off. Except for when Mom stuck in new prints, nobody ever seemed to bother to look at them.

Rose looked at them now, as the dawn grew brighter, searching fifteen years of photographs for an answer. Find out who you are, everybody was telling her.

She looked at her face smiling out of the glossy pictures. Rosecleer Potter. Maybe the question wasn't *who* are you, but something far more awful. Maybe the question was *what* are you?

As she was putting the albums back on the shelf, she heard a sound outside, a scuffling crunch of feet that made her freeze. Her first thought was: It's *him*; he's come to get me. Her second thought was not to be stupid, it was only some nocturnal animal hurrying home.

She pulled back the drapes to peep out and immediately drew back, stifling a gasp. Someone was moving furtively along the side of the house, almost close enough for her to touch on the other side of the window. She watched as he made his way toward the corner. He was going around to the kitchen.

She opened the den door a crack and listened for the sound of the kitchen door opening and closing. It came as she expected, and then the stealthy footsteps making their way into the hall and up the stairs. He knew which creaky steps to avoid, to get upstairs without making a sound.

It was the same way she went back to her room, the way she and Jerram had always sneaked around when they wanted to.

Her heart was beating painfully, and she held her breath until she was behind her own door. He hadn't seen her watching, she hoped. It seemed important that he didn't know. But why had Jerram been out? And what had he been doing?

Twenty

IT WAS SNOWING LIGHTLY ON MONDAY MORNING. Mom stood in front of the kitchen window, holding a mug of steaming coffee, rambling about how they should call a snow holiday.

Dad recognized her nervousness. "Everything's going to be fine, Liz," he said. And to Rose, "You hold your head up high, darlin'."

"I'll be fine," she said.

Jerram looked up briefly from the homework he was hurriedly scribbling to give an encouraging wink. Rose pretended not to notice. He had come down for breakfast in a perfectly normal way.

"I'm sure your friends won't act as badly as Mrs. Emerson did," Dad went on.

"Never thought I'd hear you say kids had more sense than adults," Jerram said.

Mom saw the bus through the trees on the other side of the ridge. "Five minutes."

Before Rose went out the door, Mom grabbed her and gave her a hard, brief hug. "Keep safe," she said. Rose disengaged without responding, unnerved by this sudden display of the old affection.

Grace looked pinched and unhappy when Rose sat down next to her on the bus.

"My mother's been awful," she was complaining. "Forcing me to catch up on all my homework. I'm really sorry I never called you back."

Rose was unimpressed. "What homework?" Grace had never been behind with homework in her life.

"You know how mothers can be," Grace said vaguely and looked out the window.

"Sure."

Rose stared out the window, too. It was snowing harder.

"Oh, all right, I'll tell you," Grace said suddenly. "She wouldn't let me talk to you. Something about stuff that happened in church. She acted like you were personal non whatsis . . ."

"*Persona non grata,*" Jerram put in from the seat behind. He always sat behind them, to listen in on their conversations. It had been a habit for years and had never bothered Rose until today. She felt exposed and vulnerable with Jerram at her back where she couldn't see him.

"Whatever," Grace was saying. "She acted like Rose was something contagious. What happened in church?"

"Nothing much. Mrs. Emerson called me a witch."

Grace's eyes bugged. She drew her breath in sharply. "Oh, Rose, that's awful. How did you feel?" she whispered, looking around. There was a tinge of excitement in her voice.

Rose shrugged numbly. In that moment, Grace began to move away from her, backing into a murky distance she couldn't reach anymore. Had they been growing apart before this?

"Well, it's nothing to worry about, is it? I mean, you're not a witch, are you, Rose, even if you do have some crazy ideas?"

"Thanks a lot."

"Well, you do and you know it. Not everybody understands things like entities, for instance. Who'd want to believe there were spooks floating around, like even on this bus?" Grace looked around as if she expected to see some. She frowned. "You'd better not talk about stuff like that anymore," she advised solemnly. "People could get entities mixed up with those friends witches have, what do you call them?"

"How would I know?"

"Familiars," Jerram offered in sophomoric tones.

"Yeah, like black cats," Grace said, pleased.

"We have no cats," Jerram said. "Our mother is allergic to cats. We used to have a dog but he ate the walls. He now lives in South Dakota."

"Jerram!" Grace said. "Dogs can't eat walls."

"Ours did," Jerram went on. "His name was Plastertooth. We sold him to some people heading west in a covered wagon."

They arrived at school, and Jerram abruptly ended his discourse. He had succeeded in flustering Grace. She got off the bus half huffy and half laughing, not sure if she'd been had.

But in true Grace style, she shook herself out of it and escorted Rose to the lockers. "Don't worry if anyone says anything, just ignore them," she said. It was reminiscent of Mom's advice. Ignore it. Forget it. Stick your head in the sand.

But all Rose got was some ribbing and a couple of unsure looks. For a moment she wanted to enjoy it, thinking of pretending to give them all the evil eye. Daniel stopped her.

"They're not worth it," he said. He told her how he'd come up to the house on Sunday but hadn't come in because the Reverend Joan got there first. He'd stood in the patch of woods across the road, trying to send Rose a message to come out.

"Why didn't you come in after she left?"

Daniel looked sheepish. "She saw me and said she'd take me home." He imitated the reverend's nasal voice. "'The family needs to be alone at a time like this.' I didn't know what was going on in your house, so I took the ride. I was freezing my butt by that time anyway."

Rose felt disappointed. She'd trusted him. Was he going to let her down? "Afraid she'd come to do an exorcism?" she said sharply.

He began to protest, but she interrupted. "It's okay, don't mind me. I'm gonna be late for art." She walked away.

By lunchtime, the snow was really coming down. The atmosphere in the cafeteria was festive, with everybody expecting an announcement for early closing. Grace babbled as she waited in the lunch line, pretending she was cutting Gregory dead but making sure he noticed her at the same time. Daniel was surrounded by Gregory and Company. He'd suffer merciless teasing if he and Rose sat alone together. She could tell from his face that he wanted to. She gave him a smile over the sea of heads and put a plate of lasagna on her tray.

"Rosecleer Potter?" a low, modulated voice called from the end of the line. It was Mrs. Bursack, the school secretary.

"There's someone here to see you, hon," she said, gently taking Rose's tray. "Why don't we bring your lunch into the conference room?"

Rose followed her neat, careful steps down the corridor, wondering who the visitor could be.

Mrs. Bursack nudged the conference room door open with her hip. Seated at the table, a black, fur-lined stormcoat pushed carelessly back on her shoulders, was Detective O'Hara. She looked a little disheveled, and her nose was red.

Mrs. Bursack put Rose's tray down on the conference table and said, "Be sure you eat your lunch, hon." She slipped out of the room, silent and efficient as ever. Rose sat down in front of the tray.

"Go ahead," Detective O'Hara said.

"I'm not hungry."

"We need to talk."

"We do?"

"Relax, Rose, I'm not going to bite." She reached into her big black bag for a tissue. She delicately wiped her nose.

"I don't know anything."

"About what?"

"About anything. About this . . . new girl."

"You'd tell me if you did?"

"Of course."

Detective O'Hara laughed a little, and it was obvious that her lungs were congested. Rose could smell the odor of mentholated cough drops.

"Look. Rose . . . I . . ." Her words were drowned out by the sudden crackle and static of the PA system. The principal's words came booming out above Detective O'Hara's head. Early closing. Everybody back to their homerooms now.

Rose stood up but Detective O'Hara reached out and touched her wrist. "I'll drive you home," she said. "It's okay, everything's been checked out. Get your stuff from your locker and meet me out front."

"No, thanks, I'll take the bus."

"I told you, Rose, it's been arranged."

"I don't have to go anywhere with you. Unless I'm being arrested or something. Just what I need is to leave school in a police car."

"It's not a police car. It's my gray Saab."

They glared at each other, but O'Hara won.

"We'll drive over to Benny's Diner," O'Hara said, eyeing the mess of coagulated school lasagna on the tray. "Get some coffee and a burger; what do you say?"

"Okay. I'll get my coat." As she left the room, Rose heard Detective O'Hara blowing her nose like a foghorn.

"We found Carla Fentesso this morning," O'Hara said when they were ensconced in a booth at Benny's and she had her hands cupped around a mug of steaming black coffee. It was obvious that she felt terrible, and it softened Rose a little. Not much.

"I'll be frank with you, Rose, I think you can handle it. Stab wounds in the chest and head. She was in a ditch alongside old route 7. A red plastic flower found on the body. We've traced the flowers to a theatrical supply house in New York."

"So you know who did it?"

O'Hara let out a hoarse laugh, coughed and took a sip of coffee. "Hold on. It's not as easy as that. The flowers can't talk. We still don't know who he is."

Benny brought over Rose's hamburger himself. He paused to give Detective O'Hara a long look. O'Hara stopped talking and looked back until he wiped his hands on his apron and went away.

"I know we didn't get off on the right foot," O'Hara said. "I'd like to make it different now. I hope you'll help us."

"You know what happened yesterday," Rose broke in. "I was accused of being a witch. In public, where everybody could hear. Maybe people would like to see me burned at the stake." She laughed nervously.

"I know it's been hard for you and that it could get harder," O'Hara said. "Fear can sometimes bring out the best in people, but more often the worst." Her eyes flicked toward the window where the snow was falling steadily. "Jerks," she muttered under her breath.

Rose pretended not to hear. Maybe Detective O'Hara wasn't all bad. Benny's burger was juicy and rare and when she bit into it she realized she was hungry.

"I don't know how I can help," she said, wiping

her chin. "I really mean that. Crazy as it sounds, I only get messages about where to find bodies. I have no idea who the killer is." Had Nancy's appearance at the window last night been to tell her to look for Carla on route 7? Same as usual. Dead dead dead.

"We're opening all the old cases," O'Hara was saying. "Missing girls in Bethboro, Danville and the surrounding towns. It's possible there may be more skeletons out there. This is something that's been going on for at least five years. And it could keep going on . . . unless we find him."

"Well . . ." Rose's stomach, full of hamburger, was getting queasy. "It's sort of . . . your job. The police's job to do it."

Detective O'Hara was quiet for a bit, just drinking her coffee. "Snow's getting heavy," she said finally and signaled Benny for the check.

"Chief Henning gave me this chance," she said as she rummaged in her bag for money. "He's not all that keen on psychics, you know. A politically sensitive man, our chief is. Worries a lot. Wouldn't want to be accused of pressuring you. I had to convince him it was worth a try to just ask nicely."

Rose wondered if this was the good cop, bad cop routine.

"Am I supposed to feel sympathetic?" she couldn't help asking.

"Sympathetic? Sure, you should feel sympathy. For the victims and their families, not for me." O'Hara shrugged. "Hell, I gave it my best shot."

She pulled the heavy glass door open, and they clomped out to her car, which was covered with snow. She made Rose get in while she brushed the windshield off.

O'Hara was a cop; it was her job to get information. Rose couldn't hold it against her, but she didn't like it. She felt exploited and dirty. And worried. They had found Carla this morning. But when had she been killed?

"You know," O'Hara said when she'd got in, "my family was dead set against my joining the force. I think I did it out of spite at first. I was no crusader. But now, I know I can do something worthwhile if I keep pushing myself."

The main road had been plowed, but the side roads were bad. O'Hara was a skillful driver. She maneuvered the car back in line whenever it threatened to slip. She drove confidently as she talked, not like Rose's mother who hunched nervously over the wheel and made everybody keep quiet.

"There's a DA in New York . . . does a lot for abused women, rape victims. She's on their side one hundred percent. I'd like to be like her."

"My brother would tell you to start playing the violin about now."

"Believe me or don't, Rose. The point is I'm a human being and I care about whether girls stay alive or not. I want to get this killer."

"Okay, okay," Rose cried. "But what can I do?"

O'Hara took her eyes off the road for the briefest moment to look at Rose. "Contact Nancy. Don't wait for her to come to you. Go to her."

"I . . . I don't know how to do that," Rose said truthfully. "What am I supposed to do?"

"There must be ways," O'Hara said confidently.

"There must be people who know. We could talk to them, find out what you should do."

Rose felt scared. People who know. People like the kooks they wrote about in the newspaper. People who predicted earthquakes and disasters. She didn't want to associate with them.

She was surprised to see they'd arrived at the house. O'Hara stopped the car and pulled up the hand brake. The windshield wipers clunked, the engine trembled, the snow kept coming down, the moments ticked past. O'Hara was waiting for an answer.

"I'll think about it. I mean it, I will. Just give me some time."

"That's better than nothing," O'Hara said. "Just don't take too long. We don't want another murder."

Rose sat in the warmth of the car a moment longer. "When did you . . . do you know when Carla was killed?"

O'Hara cocked her a look. "Probably some time last night. I haven't seen the medical examiner's report yet."

"I think Nancy can only tell me after they're dead, you know," she said again, as much to reiterate it to herself as to Detective O'Hara. Because if that were true, it would mean Carla was dead before Rose went to sleep, before Jerram left the house. She didn't want to think about Carla being found this morning and Jerram sneaking home. Jerram talking about research on serial killers. Jerram with his Swiss Army knife and his Totally Intact State. Jerram who never let anyone look into his knapsack. Who kept a lock on his closet door.

"You all right, Rose?"

"Yes, yes." She opened the door quickly, afraid O'Hara might read her thoughts. She got out, then leaned over into the open door. "There's something . . . I think I should tell you. But please, if it turns out to be wrong, don't let anyone know about it coming from me."

The man in the blue car was a better possibility now. She liked the idea of the man in the blue car. It was easier than thinking about Jerram. She told O'Hara.

She looked perplexed at first, but by the time Rose finished, her face was grim.

"You should have reported this right away," she said in a cold voice. She was no longer friendly. Good cop had gone. She reached over and slammed the door. The car made a U-turn, viciously throwing up snow in Rose's face. Rose watched the car speed down the hill, not skidding once.

"Sorry," Rose said, but she didn't know if she was apologizing to O'Hara or Jerram or the man in the blue car.

Twenty-one

ROSE SAT ON HER BED ALL AFTERNOON, CONCENTRATING on Nancy. She tried everything she could think of: clearing her mind, repeating a mantra, breathing control. Nancy didn't come.

And there were interruptions. A call from Grace, a call from Daniel, both wanting to know the details of being questioned by the police. Rose didn't feel like talking about it to either of them. Grace's reactions just seemed too silly now. And she felt unsure about Daniel, probably unfairly. But maybe it wasn't a good idea to tell anyone anything anymore. Nobody could really understand.

If Daniel sensed her backing off, he was cool about it. "Call you tonight?" he said, but it wasn't really a question.

She had just got back to her room when the phone rang again. She decided to ignore it, but Mom shouted up the stairs for her to answer.

There was a lot of noise on the line; then a faraway little kid's voice said, "Can you come out to play?"

"What?"

"Come out to play with me."

"Wrong number, kid," Rose said impatiently and hung up.

"Was that Jerram?" Mom called. "Just look at this storm. He should get himself home."

"No, it wasn't Jerram," Rose replied. She went back to her room to doggedly try again to reach Nancy. But she knew it wouldn't work. Maybe if she fell asleep and had a dream? But she didn't feel like sleeping. She gave up and went down to the kitchen and stuck a frozen taco in the microwave. While it nuked, she paced the kitchen. *People who knew what to do.* Detective O'Hara would want to call them, make her talk to them.

"What a case of jitters you've got," Mom said, coming up from the basement with a basket of laundry. "If you have so much nervous energy, go down and fold some wash for me."

Rose ate the taco and folded wash, then put in two more loads. The phone rang again, and she picked up the basement extension, half hoping it would be Daniel. Sweet distraction. But it was the same kid. "Come out to play," he pleaded.

"Look, you have the wrong number. Ask your mommy to dial your friend's number for you, okay?"

There was a moment of crackly silence.

"Do you understand? Ask your mommy," she repeated.

Laughter. Not little kid laughter. "My mommy's dead."

She slammed the phone down.

Just a prank. But the child's voice had sounded

so real. Using a child to make obscene calls was too creepy. Who would be sick enough to do that?

A shadow loomed suddenly against the basement wall, and she whirled around. "Jerram! You startled me."

"You were in another world. I said hello at least three times."

"Where've you been? Mom's been worrying," she said, crossly.

"At the library." He sauntered down the stairs and opened the dryer and began folding laundry with her. "Reading up on serial killers."

"What the hell for?" she snapped.

"Find out whatever I can about the way this guy might operate," he answered mildly.

"And then what?"

"Maybe track him down."

"You think you're going to do that?"

"Sure, why not? What're you so angry for?"

"I'm not angry."

"You are, too." The confused look on his face changed to a sneer. "Oh, I get it. You think you have first and only dibs on these murders. Rose the Psychic doesn't need any help."

"Don't be stupid." She carelessly stuffed the newly folded clothes into the basket. "The police are the ones with dibs."

"Now you're the one who's jealous. You don't want me infringing on your glory."

She glared at him but he stood his ground.

"Believe me, there's no glory," she said more reasonably. "Maybe I am feeling bad because I haven't accomplished very much. But God knows what you've been up to, Jerram."

"Trying to help. Isn't it obvious you need it? We should work together the way we used to. It's the only way to stop him."

"Very noble, I'm sure, but why? What has it really got to do with you?" The question was out. How would he answer? Now, looking at him, she felt ashamed to have suspected him of murdering anybody. Standing here together, folding laundry, it seemed preposterous.

Jerram was quiet for so long, she had to prod him. "Are you going to answer or what?"

"Carla Fentesso was a friend of mine."

That was a surprise. He'd never mentioned it. But Mom had said he had a friend in Westley. Carla?

"You mean . . . a girlfriend?" she asked, amazed and frightened again.

"Why not? What about Daniel?" he shot back defensively.

"Nobody's saying you shouldn't have a girlfriend. It's just that . . ." She felt bewildered. "Jerram, I don't even know you anymore."

"You said we were changing, that we have to change. You're so wrapped up in your own life, you don't really see all the changes that have already occurred. And you didn't even care when Carla was missing. You didn't want to be bothered to find out about her. I tried to explain . . . but you wouldn't listen."

"Maybe you didn't try hard enough," Rose said. "But I'm sorry, I didn't realize."

It was so much to take in. She had been wrapped up in herself, maybe she was at fault. Maybe she was jealous now, knowing Jerram had been pulling back as much as she.

"I was getting to know Carla," he said. "I didn't really want to believe she could have been killed, but I knew it was likely. I didn't think she would have gone away without telling me. So I thought if I could just find out how a guy like this thinks, maybe I could catch the bastard. I've been out for the last couple of nights, just looking for her . . . for them. I swear I'll kill him if I ever see him."

"I'm so sorry, Jerram," she said. She wanted to embrace him, but there was a new awkwardness between them.

"Anyway," he said briskly. "We need to put our heads together and figure things out. You know what Mom always says, two heads are better than one." He gave her a hesitant smile.

She told him about seeing Detective O'Hara, but Jerram knew all about it. She had talked to him in the school conference room before seeing Rose.

"Then O'Hara knew you knew Carla?"

"Why not? Her father met me. I'd been over to Westley a couple of times." His face closed up for a moment.

Jealousy threatened to flare up. He had no right to keep all these secrets from me, she thought. She tried to squelch it. "It must have been terrible, having to talk about your feelings to O'Hara."

"Yeah. We talked a lot about feelings. O'Hara wanted to know all about them." He laughed harshly. "I think she suspected I did it. Can you believe that?"

Rose felt her face burn. She covered up with reason. "That's ridiculous. You didn't have anything to do with Nancy or Cyn. My God, five years ago, when Helena Klout was killed, you were only ten years old, Jerram!" As she talked, she saw the truth in what she was saying.

"I felt the same way," he said. "But in the library I figured it out. Copycat killer, right? Maybe Carla and I had a lover's quarrel, and I decided to murder her and pass it off as just another job by the Christmas Killer."

"Not seriously." Rose didn't want to think about more possibilities. She was satisfied now. She had to be satisfied.

"Well, I didn't get arrested, did I?" Jerram's face twisted. "It was lousy. But forget it. What I wish now is that we had more to go on. Like if you'd been getting messages for the past five years instead of just since Nancy. This killer's been out there for that long."

"It brings us back to the same unanswered question. If I'm receptive now, I probably was then. So it has to be something to do with Nancy. Either she's the only victim who has the power to come back from the dead, or the only one who has wanted to."

"Or, the only one who made an impression on you."

"You mean, you think I was getting messages

from other victims but didn't realize it?"

He nodded. "You could have. You were young, maybe you thought they were just bad dreams."

"Dreams!" Rose exclaimed. "Jerram, do you still have our notebook?"

He looked puzzled, then his face cleared. "We wrote them down, didn't we?"

They hadn't thought of the notebook in years, since he'd hidden it in their old toy chest.

It was funny to see the childish handwriting. Every dream was neatly recorded, with their parts carefully labeled and dated. Jerram had been a literal child and every word had been put down.

Rose, September 21

There is a fairy godmother who knows everything. She says, "Sit down and tell me all about it." Rose won't tell. She gets scared. The fairy godmother shakes her big wand in Rose's face.

Jerram, September 21 continued

I told the fairy godmother that I don't believe in them and she said if I don't believe in them how come I am talking to one? I took out my own wand and shook it at her and she got scared and melted into a puddle of water.

"That one's obvious," Jerram said. "A nice rendition of our trips to that psychologist, the one I hated, with a little *Wizard of Oz* thrown in."

"We'd seen it on television, remember? It popped up in our dreams for months."

They read through the year to the next fall.

> *Rose, December 20*
> *A shadow comes to the window at night. It taps and asks to come in. Rose thinks: Is this a vampire? She takes a pencil out of her ear and writes a note to remind herself to buy garlic. The shadow says never mind, it will call back in an hour.*
> *Jerram, December 20, continued*
> *Rose is in her bedroom, pointing at the window. The whole place stinks like Lucky's Italian restaurant. She asks me how I like the new decorations. Garlic cloves all over. I tell her she doesn't have to worry, I'll take care of it. I grow fifty feet tall and look out the window but I don't see anything or anybody.*

"This is great stuff for a baby horror comic," Jerram said, "but it doesn't tell us much."

"I disagree," said Rose. "I had repetitive dreams about things at the window. Look what this one says: 'A creature took me in the air and over the bridge. We looked down and saw a doll lying in the water.' Couldn't that be a childish idea of seeing a dead body, thinking it was a doll? I was flying in that dream, just like I did with Nancy."

"Looks like only you had these visions of things appearing at the window. All I did was try to protect you from them."

Rose felt chastised. "You did, Jerram. You were a good brother."

He looked disheartened. "You know what these

dreams tell me? That I was only second fiddle. You were having the dreams, Rose, and inviting me in, maybe because you were scared and needed your big brother to save you. But they were your dreams, not mine."

"That's not true," she protested. "We shared our ESP, it wasn't one of us or the other. I mean, what about how you'd make me help you play your awful tricks? You had power over my mind, Jerram, you know you did."

"No. If I got you to help it was just because I was stronger than you, probably a little stinker of a bully in my own way. But you were the one who had the power. You still do. Maybe I can help, Rose, but only so far. It's up to you."

It took a few minutes for his words to sink in. "I wanted to be the same as you, Jerram. I always did. Now you're telling me we're different?"

"You have a gift and you have to use it."

"But how? How do I make it work when I need it? It's fine for all of you to ask ask ask . . . but what am I supposed to do when I don't know how to give?"

"Maybe the first step is wanting to."

"But I do want to, now that you've told me all about Carla. I want to help because of you. And, another reason. I'm starting to get crank calls. Maybe from town crackpots or . . . maybe Mom's biggest fear is coming true and they're from him, the killer. You know what? I'm not scared, I'm just angry. I want to get him. By myself."

"But we may need help."

"Yeah, O'Hara said I should talk to people who know about these things, ask them what to do, but it gives me the creeps. The only thing I can think of now is to go to Mackey's sister. He told me she could help and at least it's someone who seems normal."

"If Mackey recommended her, she's gotta be good," Jerram said, smiling a tired, sad smile.

"In the meantime, let's say nothing to Mom and Dad. Mom will only worry. Dad will get himself in a state."

Jerram took her hand. "It's down to just the two of us, then."

Rose smiled. "Just you and me again."

Part Six

Him

Dear Folks,

Only seven more shopping days until Christmas. I hope you enjoyed the gifts I sent you. Wishing you all the joys of the season.

There is one among you who knows. She will soon have the joy of blood and easeful death. May silent nights come to her. There is another among you who tells. She will soon be blessed with silence, too. The silence of death is peace.

Blessings,
Your Friend

News Story
The Bethboro-Danville Daily Standard
December 19

The number of known Christmas Killer victims hovers at four but local police say it could climb higher in the weeks to come. The body of a sixteen-year-old Danville Heights girl was exhumed yesterday to determine if the pattern of injuries match those on recent victims. The dead woman, Barbra Jean Lemmars, was found three years ago on December 24, in water beneath the Cabin River bridge. At the time, no foul play was suspected. Death was attributed to an accidental fall, or suicide. All reported cases of girls missing from the Bethboro-Danville area in November and December for the last six years are being reopened for further investigation.

The victims are Nancy Emerson, 14, Bethboro; Cynthia A. Merley, 14, Bethboro; and Carla Fentesso, 16, Westley Village. The remains of Helen Klout, reported as a runaway five years ago, were found in Danville auto yard. A signature red flower left by the killer on his victims was found near the skeleton. All victims had been stabbed or suffered fatal blows to the head. Merley was also strangled.

"There is no doubt in my mind that these killings are the work of a single individual," Bethboro police chief, Silver Henning, said in a recent interview. "This is the sickest type of perpetrator, what we call a serial killer. These girls were in the wrong place at the wrong time."

Feature Story
The Bethboro-Danville Daily Standard
December 19

What Is a Serial Killer?
An exclusive interview with Angus V. Candacy, Ph.D.
by Gary Longman, Staff Writer

He may have suffered a childhood trauma during the holiday season. Now, he kills during late November and throughout December to vent his anger at the injustices of the past. The Christmas Killer lives in a world of delusion which to him is very real. These are just some of the insights offered by Dr. Angus V. Candacy, professor of Psychology at Downstate College and author of a book on serial murderers.

Dr. Candacy believes that the Christmas Killer has revealed more than he intended in the two letters he has written to this newspaper. "He's a man with a fragile, childish ego," Candacy says. "And he's angry that he is misunderstood. He hopes to set the record straight. At the same time, he is enamored of his own importance, a dangerous combination. He's sociopathic, psychopathic but not psychotic."

Dr. Candacy explained that a serial killer is an organized, calculating person who has a time bomb of violence ticking inside. "This is not impetuous crime," Candacy says. "The serial killer plans well and derives pleasure from the crime." A serial killer usually uses the same method for all his victims and leaves some kind of message, in this case a red flower.

When asked what kind of person police should be looking for, Candacy's reply is disquieting. "Good-looking, innocent-looking, someone who could easily disarm you," Candacy replies. "This is not your stereotyped monster. When he is not killing — which is most of the time — he has a job, probably an ordinary life."

But such a person believes he is immune to laws and rules, Candacy explains. "He thinks he won't be caught," Candacy adds. "If he is apprehended, he can completely block out his guilt. He has selective amnesia."

Candacy says it's likely that this type of person gets into minor trouble, traffic violations, petty crimes. On the other hand, he could be a person everyone knows and respects.

Robert Dipthorpe, a handwriting analysis expert, concluded after a study of the first letter that obsessive-compulsive tendencies were evident in the cramped, meticulous writing.

Dr. Candacy believes the killer is asking to be caught by writing such letters.

Are there any female serial killers, this writer wonders. "They're usually poisoners," Candacy says. "Or caretakers of the sick who think they're doing their terminally ill patients a favor. But it's always possible that the Christmas Killer could be a woman. We can't rule out anything at this point."

Item
Danville Ledger
December 19

A Westley Village householder, 69-year-old Mary Wollenschaft, reported that upon return from a week's visit to her sister in Spring Farms, Massachusetts, she discovered bloodstains on her bathroom walls.

"It's the work of the Devil," Wollenschaft said when she reported it to police.

"Looks like a lot of rust to me," a neighbor who refused to give his name said. He added that Mrs. Wollenschaft had been in poor health and was nervous. When this reporter went to the premises, 896 York Hill Road, Westley, Wollenschaft refused to answer questions and turned off her hearing aid.

Westley police called in the Danville forensics department to take paint samples to determine if the stains are blood or rust.

Rose

Twenty-two

Martha Mackey's house was south of town, where there had once been a booming lumber mill. All that was left now were a few crumbling buildings, some rusting equipment and weeds. The house was up a lane behind the old mill, across the stream. The footbridge groaned as they crossed it.

"So this is Wallace Romola's romantic hideaway," Jerram said, surveying the scene.

"Miss Mackey is just a friend. You know how Wallace hates his family for what he thinks they've done to him. This is probably the only place he feels at home."

"Wallace is a crackpot, Rose, but you won't see it. What about what he's done to them? Like the time he put a bunch of baby mice inside the Thanksgiving turkey?"

"That's only a rumor and you know it."

"And the Christmas tree? He set it on fire, remember? That's no rumor because the whole fire department was there."

"Okay, okay," Rose said. "Crackpots are still human."

"How'd you like to get a spoonful of mice with your stuffing?" Jerram muttered.

The house was nondescript, a run-down split-level ranch. They picked their way through a maze of frozen flower beds. Perhaps in summer it was a riot of color, but now it looked sad and dreary.

When Martha Mackey opened the door, a powerful aroma of lemon polish and pine disinfectant blasted out from behind her. She was a small, neat woman dressed in slacks and an expensive-looking bulky sweater. Her blonde hair fell in waves to her shoulders. She wore gold earrings and bright pink lipstick. She didn't look anything like her brother.

"I've been expecting you," she said cheerfully. "Come right in."

Rose saw instantly what her mother had meant about being clean. The place was spotless. Tabletops gleamed like mirrors, floors sparkled, the rugs and upholstery had a just-washed look. Miss Mackey invited them to sit down and get comfortable.

"I'm just going to do a preliminary reading today," she said. "Then, I'll evaluate what I've learned and let you know how we may or may not proceed."

"May *not*?" Jerram asked, concerned.

"I have to see what abilities she really has," Miss Mackey said patiently. "It may be hard for you to realize, but many, many people think they have ESP when it's nothing more than a heightened sensitivity." She looked at them. "Intelligent people are most often misled. The more intelligent you are, the greater your capacity for empathy. But empathy must not be confused with true power of the mind."

Jerram looked resigned. Rose knew he was thinking: That's me, Rose. Nothing more than a good I.Q.

"We're twins, Miss Mackey," Rose said unnecessarily. "We share thoughts a lot of the time."

Miss Mackey smiled. "How can you expect otherwise, hatching from two companionable little eggs?"

"You make us sound like chickens," Jerram said.

Miss Mackey patted Rose's hand. "Tell me, dear, what is your wish? Do you want to have a special power? Or would you rather be ordinary?"

How could she answer that? How could anyone? "Whatever I am, I am," she said lamely.

Miss Mackey nodded. "That's the best answer. It means your ego is not involved. People who crave a superior specialness usually have problems."

Jerram shifted impatiently. "But Rose does have problems, Miss Mackey, that's why we came to you."

She gazed at him. "All in good time, young man."

Rose felt sorry for Jerram, knowing that what he wished most in the world was to be extraordinary.

Miss Mackey asked them to sit quietly for a few moments, to collect their thoughts. At first Rose felt fidgety, but an image began to form of her thoughts scattered about the room and she collecting them in a wicker basket, like gathering flowers.

Miss Mackey took Rose's hands in hers and studied the palms. Rose's hands began to feel hot and itchy. Miss Mackey let go and began to look at Jerram's hands. While she was doing this Rose's hands grew cool. But as soon as Miss Mackey touched them again, heat tingled up through her fingers into her arms.

"You don't have similar palms, but then you're not identical twins," she said. "Look here, Rose, this is important. Do you see this triangle formed by the lines of intuition, fate and head? This means you are unusually gifted with the power to see. Students of the occult covet such a mark. And yours has no flaws. It means a very high degree of power."

Was Rose imagining the excitement in Miss Mackey's voice? Her fingers tightened their grip on Rose until it hurt and she had to pull away. Miss Mackey looked up, startled.

"Let's try something else now," she said. "It will take a certain degree of intense concentration. I have a small mark of the seer on my own palm, and I have trained myself to engage with someone of like abilities." There was the slightest trace of pride in her voice.

She asked Rose to sit in one of two straight-backed chairs she set up facing each other in the middle of the room. She sat in the other. Their knees touched. She reached out and placed her fingertips on Rose's temples and asked Rose to do the same to her. Rose could see the fine lines etched on the pale papery skin of Miss Mackey's face, hidden only slightly by a dusting of powder. She looked much older up close.

They sat in silence, and Rose tried hard to concentrate, to go deeply into herself, as Miss Mackey asked. The sounds in the room were at first intrusive, then slowly faded. She felt sleepy, the way she did sometimes when she read in bed, drifting off and waking up with a start. She tried to resist; Miss Mackey wouldn't appreciate her taking a nap. But it was so warm and . . . the room receded into a swirl of colors, like a kaleidoscope gone mad. A sensation of dizzy falling that was not unpleasant, just that slight catch in the stomach, like when the swing used to go too high and come back down with such force you'd think to yourself that you'd discovered the secret of life, that you couldn't . . . couldn't . . . there was cold. Blackness. Emptiness. Terrible emptiness she had never known ever. A black place without sound or sensation, taste or smell. I am me, but I am not me, she thought. I am in a sea of nothingness. It was an emptiness that was final, eternal, dead.

Where are you, Rose? someone asked.

Nowhere.

Who do you see?

Nobody.

Was she supposed to see someone? Itchy reminder at the back of her mind. Someone important, someone she had to find, oh, if only she could remember who it was.

She *felt* it coming, she couldn't see because of

the blackness, a huge slug rolling toward her, with a huge maw that opened up and sucked her in. She didn't want to be here. Let me out! she shouted, and there was a roar of laughter in her ears.

What are you doing here, my little pumpkin, my little buttercup, my little peach blossom, I am going to eat you up, I am going to bite off that little nose and suck out those little eyeballs, chew on that rosy tongue. Yum yum yum.

Behind the silly singsong words there was something more dreadful. Blood and ripped flesh. Like a knife through butter, like jam on a sliced-open bun.

From far away she felt the pressure on her face. It was going to get her, eat her. Slapping her, what did she do? She came back into the room in a sudden rush of consciousness that was like a locomotive's metallic crashing. She felt angry, enraged, ready to fight back. Miss Mackey caught her thrashing hands.

"Rose, thank God, you're with us again."

Rose pulled her hands away and twisted them into her lap, feeling suddenly foolish. "Didn't know I was away," she tried to joke. Her tongue felt too big for her mouth.

"Oh, dear," Miss Mackey said nervously. "This is far beyond what I expected. I'll need some time to think, to prepare. I must do some studying."

"Are you okay, Rose?" Jerram was asking.

Like a huge carousel grinding to a halt, the room ceased spinning, the furnishings and colors shuddered and stopped.

"I feel fuzzy. But yes, I think so. What happened?"

"You went away," Miss Mackey said, her face ashen. "You regressed to another place entirely. I'm not even sure you were breathing. My goodness, I was worried."

Jerram looked annoyed. "Of course she was breathing. What are you trying to do, scare her?"

"No, no, not at all. But this is strong, much more potent than I've ever seen. Rose, dear, you must do some work, too, before we can meet again."

Bewildered, Rose asked, "Do what?"

Miss Mackey hesitated. "You . . . need to find out more about yourself. There is a powerful connection between you and . . . oh, dear. . . ." She looked helplessly at Jerram who simply stared back. ". . . between you and the dead."

Jerram snorted. "Well, we knew that."

Miss Mackey put her hand on his arm. "No, Jerram, we didn't know. This isn't ordinary. Rose isn't simply a sensitive medium for receiving messages. There's something more to it. And Rose must find out what it is."

"And if she finds out?" Jerram asked.

"I'll have to consider carefully, but we might try a full regression."

"And is that something that could be dangerous to Rose?"

"Well, yes, I must be truthful. It could be. But we'll take every precaution."

"I don't know about that — " Jerram said.

"Stop it, both of you!" Rose cried. "How dare you talk about me like I'm some kind of . . .

thing? I'll decide what I want to do. In the meantime you'd better remember that I'm alive, and I have a brain. I'm not some laboratory rat you can experiment with."

Two spots of color appeared on Miss Mackey's pale cheeks. "My dear, I never intended — "

"Rose is right," Jerram said. He helped Rose out of the chair. "Come on, we've had enough mumbo jumbo for one day."

"Take some time," Miss Mackey said, seeing them to the door. "Think about it, and come to see me again."

"That's up to Rose," Jerram told her. Rose said nothing. She just wanted to get out of there.

But Miss Mackey's voice reached them as they were going over the footbridge. "Find out who you are, Rose," she called. The words hung in the air.

Rose felt loathsome. She felt contaminated. But not just with the dead. There was something else. Something evil. It had touched her, embraced her. She had been inside it. What she wanted now was a bath. She would scrub herself raw because she could still smell the breath of the worm on her skin, she could taste his saliva.

She had been inside somebody's mind.

Twenty-three

"MURIEL PHONED," MOM SAID WHEN THEY ARrived home. "She left a message. 'It's on again.' She said you'd know what it was about."

The man from New York, it had to be, Rose thought; he was coming after all. Muriel had gone to New York for a few days, to go to the theatrical costumers and settle the problem with the tap costumes in person. The hats were too heavy for the little kids to dance in, and the batons were so flimsy, they bent after one rehearsal. Maybe she saw him when she was there, and persuaded him to change his mind.

Rose started for the phone but Mom stopped her. "One moment, young lady. And you, too, Jerram. Don't try to slink away. Just where have you been?"

Rose and Jerram looked at each other. "Why?" Jerram asked.

"Don't ask me *why*!" Mom said. Her voice was shrill.

"But it's broad daylight, and it's Christmas vacation, and Rose and I have just been out. What's the big deal all of a sudden?"

Mom tapped her foot. "You have not just been out. You've been up to something."

"We're not babies anymore," Jerram said, opening the refrigerator. Mom pushed it closed again.

"Mom, what's this about?" Rose asked.

"Honesty is what it's about. Telling the truth, sharing the problem. Family rules."

"There is no problem," said Jerram trying again for the refrigerator door. He yanked out a can of juice. But Mom wasn't paying attention. She was nervously folding and unfolding a dish towel, and it was obvious that she was not so much angry as just plain upset.

"Both of you can stop treating *me* like a baby," she said. "Why can't you tell your own mother what you tell the police?"

"We have," Rose said.

"Don't lie, Rose."

"I'm not lying."

"Then why did Silver Henning phone to tell me that they have a lead on that blue Dodge? What blue Dodge? What do you think you're playing at?"

"What did the police find out?" Jerram and Rose blurted out together.

"You answer my question first, please."

"Rose just saw some car that looked suspicious," Jerram said offhandedly.

"The car she saw when we bought the tree? The man she said knew your father? Don't treat me like an idiot. Somehow Rose has come into contact with this maniac killer, and you're both acting as if this were some TV show. Well, let me tell you this is not television, you two are not detectives, and this man is dangerous."

"We know he's dangerous, Mom," Jerram said.

"Do you?" She looked at Rose. "You especially are behaving like a silly little girl. You think you have some kind of power that's going to make you immune?" Rose had never seen her mother so coldly and intently furious.

"You're just as vulnerable as Nancy and Cynthia and the rest. You're nothing special, Rose," Mom screamed. "You're just an ordinary human being!"

She stopped and took a breath, then got herself a glass of water at the sink.

"But Rose isn't ordinary — " Jerram began to say.

"She is! Both of you are ordinary. You're just kids, naive kids who — " There was a rapping at the kitchen door. "God, who's that?" Mom said more quietly.

Jerram took a look. "It's Barney. Should I let her in?"

"Tell her to go to hell," Mom said. She slammed the glass of water down on the counter and stomped out of the kitchen. Jerram and Rose just stared at her back, stunned. The rapping continued.

"We'd better do something," Rose said.

"Hi, there," Barney said when Jerram opened the door. Her nose was twitching with the scent of gossip. "Just thought I'd say hello, see how you all are doing."

She tried to take a step inside but he blocked her way. "We're fine."

"Oh? That's good, then. Having a nice vacation?"

"It just started, Mrs. Barnes."

"Yes, that's right." Her eyes darted around the kitchen. "Your mother home?"

"She's busy right now."

"Well, guess I'd better get on my horse!" She turned away, then back again. "Oh, did you hear? They found blood all over some old lady's house in Westley." Jerram winced at the mention of the town, but Barney didn't notice.

"And she has a strange man living with her," Barney added in a conspiratorial whisper.

"Really?" Jerram whispered back. Barney looked gratified. Jerram managed to inch her out and firmly shut the door.

Jerram shook his head. "I read about that in the paper. It was only some old rust stains in the bathroom." He laughed. "The strange man is her tenant, some salesman whose been there for years."

Rose left him in the kitchen and went to find Mom. There were important questions that needed to be asked.

Mom was lying down on her bed, something she hardly ever did during the day. The room was shadowy; she'd pulled the drapes closed. "I have a headache, Rose," she said.

"I need to talk to you. It's really important."

Mom sighed and patted the bed next to her.

"I'm sorry for not telling you about the car. I know it was stupid of me," Rose said.

"Yes it was. But I should apologize, too. I just lost it for a moment. I shouldn't have yelled."

"All this has us upset."

"It's not only that."

"Yes," Rose said. "I know."

She sat up then. "What do you know?"

"I know there's something different about me. Isn't there?"

"Oh . . ."

"There is, isn't there? You can't keep hiding it from me, Mom. You've got to tell me."

"Don't give me orders, Rose."

"Mom, please!"

She smiled a tentative, painful smile. "Why is it so important?"

"Don't you already know? The dreams, the messages from Nancy. It's scary. Seeing Nancy's face at my window, seeing her in school, like she's standing right there. And, other things, too."

Hesitantly, she related the visit to Miss Mackey's. But she couldn't bring herself to tell it all. Not everything. Not being inside that . . . she gave her mind a shake. "I couldn't share all this," Rose said, "because I didn't know it all until now. Until Miss Mackey told me that I had to find out what made me different."

Mom looked away, her lips a thin, angry line. "So you want to believe her instead of your own mother?"

Rose reached out but Mom pulled back. "Mom! I have to know the truth, and you have to tell me. What about honesty and sharing now? Who's not following the rules now?"

"Keep your voice down," she said. "This isn't easy for me."

Rose wasn't sympathetic. "Do you think it's easy for me?"

"No, I'm sure it's not. But you have to understand, I wasn't trying to hurt you, Rose. I never thought any of it would matter. It was something that happened long ago, nothing to do with you. Or so I thought. When you and Jerram began to have those dreams I worried a little, but Dad bought the books, and there was a perfectly logical explanation for it all. Twins did things like that, shared thoughts and secrets. Some twins even had secret languages nobody else could understand. It wasn't until now that it all came back again."

"What is it, Mom? Tell me."

She touched Rose then, but in a tentative, almost frightened way. Then she hugged herself, closed herself in.

"When I was pregnant . . . I knew I was carrying twins. We were so excited when we found out. We had to go back and buy doubles of everything. Two for the price of one, Dad said." Mom smiled. "We felt lucky, Rose. We wanted both of you so much. And then something happened." She paused distractedly and looked toward the window for a few long moments.

Rose waited. Give her time. Let her get it out at her own speed, even though it was hard to listen patiently.

"In the seventh month . . . a heartbeat . . . one of the heartbeats stopped. One night, I was brushing my teeth and there was this little jolt inside me. I leaned against the sink because I felt dizzy, and I got this strange sensation, like a buzzing inside and then . . . it was as if one of you had left. It sounds like nonsense, but that's the impression I had, that one of you had just gone. Your father made me lie down and insisted on phoning the doctor even though it was past eleven. The doctor said it was probably only indigestion.

"But the next day the feeling was still there and I argued to get an appointment with the doctor. And when he finally examined me, he heard only one heartbeat. He told me one of my babies was dead."

Her voice caught, and Rose thought she would cry, but she went on with dry eyes. "We had to wait to decide what to do. There was a possibility of danger to the other twin. It was terrible to know I was carrying two little bodies, one alive and one dead. They were going to do a cesarean, but it was just a bit too early." She gripped Rose's hands now. "I wished so hard, Rose. I would have done anything for it to be all right again, for that little heart to start beating." She looked up with tear-shined eyes. "And, of course, it did! When they all thought there was no use, that it was final, your heart started beating, and you were alive again."

"Me? It was me who was dead?"

"Oh, yes, it had to be you. Don't you understand? I do now. You went wherever it is we go when we die. You've been there, and you've come back. That's why Nancy can talk to you, and you can get messages from the dead. Because, in a way, you're one of them."

"Mom, I'm alive. How can I be *one of them*?"

"You *died,* Rose. You're alive now, but you've been dead. Now you can tell Miss Mackey you found out who you are. A person who knows what's there, on the other side. You spent time there, Rose! I'm frightened for you."

"You're not supposed to be frightened! You're supposed to be my mother, tell me what to do, make it all right again!"

Mom just looked at her tearfully. Mom didn't have all the answers. Loneliness fell over Rose like a shroud. She felt as if she were moving fast through blank space, a black place pinpricked by stars, moving toward a nothingness she knew well. She saw herself alone in the vast sea of the cosmos. And at the same time, it was as if the universe were contained within her.

She went, halfheartedly now, to phone Muriel. Life had to go on, and there was still a future. Maybe this man from New York would offer her an instant scholarship and she could leave Bethboro, leave everybody and just go her own way.

The phone rang as she reached for it.

"The time will come," said the hollow voice, "to talk of many things: Of limbs and hearts and sealing wax, of ravages and kings. And why the blood is boiling hot, and whether pigs have wings."

"*Alice in Wonderland,*" Rose said.

"You're wrong!" the voice replied viciously. "*Through the Looking Glass,* little blossom. Think about it. You'll get it."

He slammed the phone down before she could.

Rose pushed down for a dial tone and punched

in the number of the Bethboro police. They could trace calls, couldn't they? They could get him if he called again.

Detective O'Hara and Chief Henning were not available, but Sergeant Blake was glad to help.

"On a crank call," he said, "the best thing to do is hang up."

"Crank call?" Rose said slowly. "You think it's just that?"

"What can you do? People are sick," Sergeant Blake commiserated. "Try not to let it get you down; they'll get bored before long and pick on someone else."

"But will you give the message to Detective O'Hara, anyway?"

"Will do. She'll look into it, don't worry your head."

Rose went to take the bath she had promised herself. She sat in the tub for a long time, thinking crazy thoughts. She wondered how it was to float in a prenatal fluid, to die and be reborn again.

Little Blossom. Sealing Wax. Pigs. It was *him.* Little Blossom was Rose. Sealing wax had been on the letters to the newspaper. Pigs were cops. He was mocking the police. Whether pigs have wings. Whether or not they could catch him.

And like Alice, she was going to go through the looking glass to find out who he was.

How could he know that?

Twenty-four

THE TELEPHONE HAD BECOME AN INSTRUMENT OF torture. After Muriel phoned to tell her the man from New York would be at the recital, there was no one else Rose wanted to hear from, except maybe God who would tell her that Nancy and the Christmas Killer were just part of a bad dream and she could wake up now.

Muriel had been effusive and excited, more bubbly than Rose had ever remembered her being. She'd been to New York and had exchanged the tap routine hats and batons. Lighter hats for little kids' heads, heavier batons to stand up against little kids' mischief. And she had seen and talked to the "someone" who had agreed to come up for the recital especially to see Rose.

"He's very interested in you," Muriel said.

"Who is this someone?" Rose asked, hoping Muriel would say he was connected with the American Ballet Theatre.

"It's a surprise," Muriel bubbled. "I'm so happy," she added before Rose said good-bye.

"This is going to be the best Christmas I've had in a long time."

Talking to Daniel was suddenly a strain, because she kept wondering if she would ever have a normal life with someone like him. What about her children? What if this thing was in her genes, would make them vulnerable, too? Was communication with the dead an inheritable disease? Marriage, children, was it Rosecleer Potter talking, she wondered? Her future had always seemed clear, a beeline to the ABT in New York. Her feelings for Daniel confused her, made her think about a life without dance, made her angry for thinking it, as if he were putting obstacles in her path. She made excuses. It seemed important that he stay away. She didn't want him to see her going through the looking glass.

And Grace. Grace had taken to sneaking phone calls, whispering her conversations, in case her mother found out she was talking to Rose. Rose felt betrayed. Grace's mother had known her since she was a little kid, had baked her cookies, put peroxide on scraped knees, once gave Rose the best prize at Grace's birthday party even though Rose hadn't done a good job on pin-the-tail-on-the-donkey.

"I can come over," Grace said. "I'll tell her I'm going somewhere else."

"Not today," Rose said, "I don't feel well. I think I'm having a relapse of the flu."

"Poor you," Grace sympathized. "Whoops, here she comes, gotta go!"

Detective O'Hara called back. She didn't think it was just a crank call. She asked a lot of questions.

"It was him," Rose said. "He knew things." How could she explain?

"Next time he calls, try to get more information," O'Hara said and Rose laughed inwardly, imagining herself asking for an address and telephone number. They would see about tracing calls, but in the meantime the police assured the Potters that patrol cars were keeping watch. Mom was skeptical. She looked out the window hourly and muttered, "I don't see any of these famous patrol cars."

Jerram was the only constant. He was solid as a rock. "You can bag it," he said. "Don't put yourself through it, if you don't want to."

"No, I want to do it, I've got to get it over with," Rose told him.

They were going to Miss Mackey's, and they would do the regression.

Whether Mom knew or not was beside the point. Rose felt Mom didn't have a say in it now. Nor Dad. She had tried to talk to him about it, after Mom told her what happened before her birth. Dad had always seemed easy to talk to so Rose was astonished at the way he acted now.

"We don't need to be talking about that, darlin'," he said uncomfortably, looking at her over the top of his reading glasses.

"But don't you see, it could be the answer to everything about what's happening to me."

"Your mama," he said, harking back to the way he used to refer to her when Rose was a baby, "she gets these ideas. I'm sorry she discussed it with you, to tell the honest truth. Because I don't think there's any sense in it."

"It might be connected to my getting messages from the dead."

"Now, we don't know that," Dad said. "And what we don't want to do is get carried away by conjecture. Act on the facts. Dreams are not facts."

Rose didn't understand. "You defended me against Mrs. Emerson, against Reverend Fairley!" she said to him.

"And I'm defending you now," he said quietly.

Jerram kept trying to cheer her up as they took the shortcut through the woods to Martha Mackey's house. The day was grim, with a leaden overcast sky. Thomas Hardy would have loved it.

"We should have brought bread crumbs," Jerram joked. "This is just like 'Hansel and Gretel.'"

"Yeah, complete with the wicked stepmother," said Rose.

"Don't be so hard, Rose. It's not Mom's fault."

"Part of it isn't. The other part I'm not so sure. Her being scared makes me scared. I always thought a mother could protect you from anything. But, listen, thanks for being here through it all. Nobody else would understand the way you do."

"Not even Daniel?" Jerram asked tensely.

"I don't want him involved in this. This is private, for family," Rose said, and Jerram relaxed.

"I'm not all good," he reminded her. "I have my own personal reasons for wanting to get this killer."

They fell into silence, and there was only the sound of their footsteps through the layers of leaves, or the sudden snap of a twig. As they came out behind the old mill, a figure loomed up.

"It's only Wallace," Rose said.

Jerram was annoyed. "He's not going to sit in on this thing, I hope."

Wallace acknowledged them with a nod. He was busy rummaging through a stack of rusted cans and broken tools. He said nothing as they made their way past him toward the footbridge. Then he called out to Rose. "Miss!"

"Keep going," Jerram urged, but Rose said they'd better wait. Wallace was sensitive to what he thought were snubs. She stopped and Wallace took a few steps toward her. He glared at Jerram until Jerram retreated out of earshot.

"It's a trick of mirrors," Wallace said elliptically. He was in bad shape today, looking more threadbare and thinner than usual. His beautiful blue eyes were red. He seemed greatly troubled. "I've been a long time watching and have no other way to explain. It's her turned into another."

"Who, Wallace?"

"The dark dancer, who else? She who would take on the aspects of another kind. It could be a miracle."

"Could you explain a little more?"

But this distressed him, and she was afraid he would go into one of his fits. It was best to humor him and think about it later, if it made any sense at all. "Thank you, Wallace," she said calmly. "It was very nice of you to tell me."

His mouth worked. Little drops of spittle flew.

"Yin and yang, light and dark. A look in the mirror reflects the same." He seemed aware that Rose didn't understand. "Like you." He pointed at Rose. "Like him." He gestured toward Jerram. "One is the shadow of the other." His feet began an agitated dance.

"Come on, Rose!" Jerram called.

"Many worries I have had," Wallace whined. "Many bad hurts. Would I do that?"

"Good-bye, Wallace," Rose said gently and slowly walked back to the bridge.

"What was all that about?" Jerram asked.

"I'm not sure."

Wallace's voice suddenly rang out in the still woods. "One good, one evil!"

Wallace pointed at them, and Rose shuddered.

"Pay no attention," Jerram said, hurrying Rose along.

"He's trying to say something about . . . twins. Don't run. He gets upset when people run away from him."

"Hard cheese," Jerram said dismissively. "He's totally crazy, Rose, no matter what you think."

Miss Mackey was at the door, looking toward Wallace with concern. "He's not at all well. It's this stress over the murders. He frets about the police suspecting him. It's so unfair when the poor man is innocent."

"You're sure he is?" Jerram asked, looking back

to where Wallace was waving his arms and circling the junkpile in a grotesque dance.

"Of course!" Miss Mackey said. "Wallace has his own modest psychic powers, you know. He feels things deeply."

She brought them into the living room. The two straight-backed chairs were arranged as they had been before. But now there was a Christmas tree in one corner, decorated in silver and red, the tinsel shimmering with the changing light, the ornaments tinkling slightly. The effect was comforting yet incongruous, as if life were the same, yet everything was different.

"You're a brave girl, Rose."

"I don't feel very brave. It's just something I have to do. To get some answers."

"Then let's hope that's what we accomplish," Miss Mackey said. "Jerram, stand behind Rose's chair and be her anchor. Keep your hands on her shoulders. As she goes deeply into a trance, we must be here to make sure she comes back."

"What do you mean 'comes back'?" Jerram's voice was anxious but wary.

"I only meant, so she can come out of it when she wants to."

"Are you sure this is safe?" he asked.

Miss Mackey looked irritated. "Yes, yes. But when you work with the mind, there's always the chance of an upset. We'll be here to make sure Rose isn't frightened."

Jerram looked dubious. "Rose? You want to go along with this? Maybe we should have a doctor or something?"

"No, we don't want doctors!" Miss Mackey said

adamantly. "They have no imagination. They don't believe."

Rose listened to them, a little nervous but amused.

"It's all right, Jerram," she told him. She hadn't come this far to stop now.

Miss Mackey looked relieved. "Good. Now let us begin."

The time has come, Walrus, Rose thought, to find out many things. Perhaps the Rose will blossom.

Twenty-five

CRACKED MEMORIES. A STIFF DRY THROAT. A LEAF pushing, torn out of spring. Rose climbed into the river that was time and went to sleep, drifted on the current that was neither backwards nor forwards but moving in a loop of forever. After a while, she arrived at a distant shore and went walking to the brink of herself.

Felt as if the shell had opened and the two halves of delicate nutmeat were splitting apart to be eaten separately by the wolves of eternity.

I have leaned against you, Jerram, she thought, and I have become you. Now I will become me.

And in becoming, she dreamed the journey.

So that I won't forget, so that in a moment of forgetfulness it won't slip my mind that I am existing still, I must leave a mark on each tree, to find my way back again, I will carve my initials in the brown bark. This is like a dream yet not, moving through the forest of night in the nearly evening, a bread-smelling granite meadow spreads itself out under the tides of night. Everything is familiar. Everything smells of endless othertimes.

First moving very fast through the trees, then through a cold-spired city of clockless cobbles and people without faces; then out into a vast corridor of space. A woman is walking in front of me. She walks and I walk. Coming up close behind her I can see she is old but has fine gold hair. Could I whisper in her ear? She seems unconcerned with my presence next to her, somehow expects it. Windowlights in the sky look into endless elsewheres, or perhaps it is the elsewhere looking in at me. She is walking toward the ramparts of a dream castle that slithers in inconstancy, like the quicksilver marks left by clouds across the sun. Without speaking she points to a doorway. I must go through. My first living thought in the hour of my birth is "What do I remember?"

The door is heavy but strangely warm; it pulsates with dusky life, it moves silently but heavily at my touch, then closes behind me with a sucking thump.

I am in a place beyond where the sun shines, a place the moon has forgotten, where fire has never burned, where music is silent and voices mute. Thoughts are not thought here, time is never wound, words are never written, never read. I am on the shores of nowhere waiting by a sea that is not green. In the background of the gauzy air is a continuous and rhythmic beating.

Oh, help.

Then endless space takes on limitations and feels safe again. An amber tinge in what might be a sky. And somehow I begin to remember this place.

"What are you doing here, Rose?"

Nancy's voice comes from nowhere and everywhere. The far horizon blossoms into mauve and pink.

"Are you dead, Rose?"

"I was dead once."

"You can't be here unless you're dead now."

"I came to ask an important question."

"We have no need for answers here."

"But you must help me, Nancy."

Her laughter sets the waves rippling. The beating quickens for a moment, then settles back, like the beating of a heart.

"Help me the way I helped you, Nancy. Remember?"

The laughter stops. "I don't mean to be cruel. It's just that you wouldn't understand."

"Where are you? Why can't I see you?"

"This is a waiting place, Rose. It only lasts a moment in the long unfolding of the universe. We don't stay here."

"It will only take a moment. Tell me who he is, the man who . . . who killed you."

"Why, I don't know, Rose. What made you think I could tell you that?"

"But you must know, you must help. We have to stop him."

"I saw his face but I didn't recognize him." Her voice is detached, unconcerned. She has changed again, now less Nancy and more of something else.

"The others . . . are they here? Helen and Carla and your friend Cyn? Maybe they can tell me?"

"I don't know if they can talk to you."

"If you can, why not them?"

"It's not a thing everyone can do, Rose." She sounds solicitous, almost motherly.

"Please help me. If you don't, he'll just go on and on. He might kill me."

"But you see," she says, "it doesn't concern me anymore."

"It concerned you once. You came to me, Nancy. Why did you do it if you didn't care?"

There is a long silence. "Yes, it's true. I did care. I can remember feeling that."

"Then let me talk to them."

"You can't stay here, Rose."

"I'll stay as long as it takes to get the answer."

"Oh, I wouldn't do that, Rose. It wouldn't be a good idea. Changes occur here."

"Nancy, can you please speak plainly? Am I in danger here?" It is hard to imagine this place as dangerous, with the sea gently lapping in time to the beating of the vast protective heart of sky.

"No," she says unsurely, as if it is hard for her to speak in ordinary terms. "Nothing will harm you."

"Then I'll stay."

"You will do what you will do," she says enigmatically. "And the changes will come in their own sweet time if they come at all."

"And the other girls? Will they talk to me?"

There was no answer. "Nancy? Nancy!"

I am alone on the shore. Time loops and slides in my mind; moments pass, or perhaps it is days. The far clouds move across the kaleidoscope horizon, changing from pink to purple to blue. The sea turns to silver. The heartbeat soothes me, lulls me, protects me. I feel as if I could lie down and sleep forever.

"Don't go to sleep, Rose," Nancy's voice warns.

But I am tired and so at peace. A change in the light wakes me. The shapes blur into view against the sky.

"I've brought them," Nancy says. "But it's only Carla and Cyn. The others . . . it's not possible for them. They've already gone."

I can't see their faces. There is just the amorphous blending and unblending of their shapes and the feeling of their being there. And something else. A peace emanating from them. It helps me remember. There was something more important, something I always knew I had to do. Something I'd stupidly put aside and forgotten and now. . . .

"Pay attention, Rose," Nancy says sharply. "It's hard for them to speak to you. They didn't want to come."

"I'm sorry." I wish I could see their eyes, touch their hands.

"None of us knows him," Nancy says. "But we will try to help you. We don't remember some things anymore, we don't know the words to use."

I need to concentrate very hard to understand them. They have indeed forgotten words, they are speaking another tongue.

"He was kind-faced, like a father man. He spoke softly," one says.

"Yes, kind but he took me to that place and cut my flesh with a sharp knife. A bright blade that hurt," says the other.

"Then he smiled and said my blood was beautiful."

"The blood ran all over the room, onto the floor and into the cracks in the walls. He put his fingers in it, licked them clean."

"Where was this room?" I ask. "What did it look like?"

"A room in a town," they say vaguely. My hopes fall. Their voices half sing, half chant, words like a liturgy for their suffering.

"If only you could tell me something more," I plead.

"He was like the dark dancer. He said she had wronged him badly, a long time ago."

"Yes, you know that face," Nancy said. "You told me on the road home in the cold moment when you comforted me. You have seen that face and were not afraid."

"But he cut us with a knife and our flesh opened and the blood ran. . . ."

"And so our lives ended."

My heart is filling up with their pain. I am hurting inside with their wounds, crying their tears. This seems a cruel thing I am doing. Or am I trying to save myself? "It's all right, it doesn't matter." I feel the sobs of dreams, when you think your heart will break out of joy or sadness, you can hardly know which.

Someone, something, strokes me, comforts me with an enveloping warmth. If this is death, then death is kind. It is only sleep and peace.

Poor piglet, I remember. "Nancy, why were you crying?"

"I'm not crying," Nancy says. "You are only feeling the things we are leaving here on the shore. We are going now."

But I must know.

"Not now, then, long ago when you were alive. Tell me, please. Because it was the trouble you were in that somehow linked you to me."

"No, Rose, it was you who linked your heart in a moment of love. The trouble was some small thing of a girl's life. In the linear time that ruled, I was late." Nancy's laughter rippled over the water like slivers of crystal. "You believe time to be so important. A few moments lost here or there and anger follows. You must see how silly that is, Rose."

"Yes." Yes. My perception of time was fading. All that, back there, seemed to be unimportant. I wanted to laugh with Nancy, to feel my soul cracking open like smashed crystal. Perhaps it was only that she was out too late and was afraid of her mother's anger. Yes, it is silly, Nancy. Here, walking near the quiet fingers of slow rivers, where eternal wind sweeps into cosmic passageways, the sun shines upon me and I am no longer trapped by time. In a moment now, I will walk into one of the passageways. I will disappear and reappear forever.

"Rose, Rose, Rose." Someone is calling me, like an irritating barb I try to push out of my mind.

"Rose, come back!"

No, I want to stay. A lovely light is dawning in the sky; the sea has changed to gold.

Nancy and Cyn and Carla are flowing toward

the clouds. I want to go with them. In a moment I will see their faces. See their smiles.

I reach out and almost grasp their hands.

But Nancy is pushing me back. "Go away now, Rose. This is not the way for you."

"But it's all right," I say, enveloped in tenderness.

Nancy pushes harder, and I feel a sharp pain in my shoulder. "Go back! Your brother is calling you."

Yes, now I recognize Jerram's voice, coming through the golden light, growing louder and stronger.

"Leave me alone," I shout back at him, resisting, willing myself into the memoryless waters of the golden sea. I would move into the spiral arms of the galaxies, past jewel-clustered stars, through the great gasbright lights of Orion, to the other side of my beginning, where I would begin again. I knew this. I have always known this.

"Go away!" Nancy says. "This is not your time to die. You have things to do yet. You will use the gift, you will find *him* and you will destroy him, and yet he will come again for you and you will kill him in the end but only after long years have passed."

Nancy is saying good-bye. Wait. "Who? Tell me who!"

"The man who kills at Christmas, he will be your shadow dancer until he is finished. You are like two halves of what can never be put together. One good, one evil. Good-bye, Rose."

"Wait, Nancy," I say, but she pushes and I fall, like Alice down the rabbit hole. I feel myself yanked down a long, slick, dark tunnel, headlong toward the opposite end of the kaleidoscope lens. There is a moment of terror and the smell and taste of blood, before I am pulled into air and blinding light.

I hear screaming: a wail, half angry, half joyous, like a baby at birth. I feel a terrible regret. In that split second change from dark to light I remembered it all. And now, in the hour of my birth, I have again forgotten.

Miss Mackey was rubbing Rose's hands. Jerram was sticking a glass of brandy under her nose. She coughed and spat and pushed it aside.

"Oh, thank God," Miss Mackey said. "I thought we'd lost you."

Jerram said nothing. He was looking at Miss Mackey in an oddly hostile way.

"We must ask, you understand," Miss Mackey said. "I know it's a shock, but it's in these first crucial moments that you'll remember most. What happened? What did you find out?"

Rose opened her mouth but no words came. Jerram was solicitous. "Take it easy. We'll get you home," he said, but Miss Mackey kept shooting questions at her.

"You did contact someone, didn't you? You were there, on the other side? Is there life after death? What was it like? Did they say anything? Did they say who the killer was? Was it Wallace?" Miss Mackey's face crumpled with dread. "Oh, they didn't say it was Wallace, did they?" she keened.

Jerram exploded. "Is that all you wanted? To

make sure your precious crackpot was innocent? It's unconscionable. Rose might have died."

"Oh, no, oh, no," Miss Mackey said. "You have it all wrong."

"I don't think so. I heard you asking when Rose was in that trance, begging her to find out about Wallace."

"But it wasn't just for that," Miss Mackey cried as Jerram helped Rose to the door. "It wasn't that at all."

"Can you walk?" he asked Rose. "Should I phone a cab?"

She felt weak and exhausted but just wanted to get into the open air.

"You have misunderstood," Miss Mackey said, becoming dignified. "I helped Rose, regardless of what you think. No one else could have helped her. No one else has the power."

"Rose is the only one with the power," Jerram said.

"No, don't," Rose said. She pressed Miss Mackey's hand. "It's all right."

"Thank you, dear," she said. "Don't blame me for asking about Wallace. I have known and cared for him since he was a child. His family has always treated him like an outcast. You go home and rest now, and when you feel better perhaps you'll come back and tell me all about it."

I don't know what to tell, Rose thought. I haven't accomplished what I set out to do. All I have is the bad taste of something like a curse. A far distant feeling of a dread that will go on.

"Good-*bye*, Miss Mackey," Jerram said.

Once they were across the bridge and into the

woods, Rose had to sit down. "You're feeling better," Jerram observed. "You're smiling."

"Am I? How odd. I don't feel like smiling. I feel so serious inside. I think I learned something very important, something about death and life. Two sides of the same coin. I'm not afraid to die. But there's something I think I should fear. I just can't remember what it is."

He frowned. "Well, unfortunately you didn't come back with a composite sketch of the killer, so he's the same threat he was before all this." He added hesitantly. "She . . . Carla . . . did she give you some message for me?"

"I'm sorry, Jerram."

He shrugged. "It was just a thought. Maybe you don't find death anything to be afraid of now, but Carla and the rest of the girls, they didn't have to die that way. They must have been frightened."

"Let me think about it. I might remember something. I have a feeling at the back of my mind that I know. It keeps teasing me. I just need some time."

"Take all the time you need," he said. "Only make sure it doesn't take too long."

Rose felt sad. Jerram felt helpless and still jealous. He wanted to be the one to avenge Carla. He had counted on her coming back with the answers. He really wasn't very different from Miss Mackey. Both of them were concerned about someone they loved. How could you blame them for that?

Part Seven

Him

SOMETIMES I LIKE TO SIT IN THE DARK AND TELL myself Christmas stories. 'Twas the days before Christmas and all through the house, not a body was stirring not even a corpse.

Christmas. Why is everyone always so happy? My Christmas story is not happy. Long ago, mothertimes, I was happy. *Don't look at the presents,* Mother said. *Don't peek.* But small boys like to peek. Just a glimpse of the goodies reassures them.

Don't look, Mother said, *I mean it.* Small boys peek anyway. They can't resist. Small boys are bad and deserve to be punished.

Mother punished. Tied the boy up in the dark cellar where things run on the floor and snuffle in corners.

Mother brings the puppy down to the cellar in a silver box tied with red ribbons. *This is what happens to boys who peek,* Mother says. *Their Christmas presents die.*

The small boy looks at the small dog body lying in tissue, small dog eyes staring. Mother leaves them in the cellar together so they can meditate on their sins.

The sister blamed it all on the boy. Wouldn't listen. Thought the boy killed the puppy in the dark cellar. Christmas became ever after as dark as that cellar, reminding them.

After a time, it was necessary to bring back the light. The boy, older now, brought light into Christmas. He made flames as bright as summer as the Christmas tree burned, and the Mother burned.

Soon learned blood is better than fire. Blood flows quietly, secretly and glows red.

I was afraid of her. Now I am strong. I will make a beautiful red Christmas. She will know the real me, and she will forgive me.

Rose

Twenty-six

CHRISTMAS WAS LIKE WALKING ON EGGS. DANIEL sent her a gold chain and a note: "I'm here if you need me." The telephone was mercifully silent, except for Muriel phoning to set up a rehearsal the following Wednesday. Muriel's voice conveyed the same bubbly excitement it had the last time she and Rose spoke. "This Christmas might just be a miracle," she said. "Someone very special is going to spend it with me."

"I'm glad," Rose said and meant it. Muriel deserved something special. Rose had a feeling Muriel had put in her time in Bethboro, working out some old problem.

"I'm gladder," Muriel said. "I've misjudged someone very dear to me. I've been very wrong."

"I hope I don't get the recital wrong," Rose said. "After all the trouble you've gone through."

"One good thing leads to another," Muriel said. "See you Wednesday. Come early. There are no classes, we'll have lunch together."

"Okay. Merry Christmas."

"You, too. It will be the first merry one for me in a long time."

On Tuesday, the day after Christmas, Grace decided she was coming over. Her mother was willing to concede, in the spirit of Christmas, that it wasn't right to listen to malicious gossip.

"I'll be bringing your present," Grace said, and Rose realized she'd forgotten to buy Grace a gift. The trip to the mall seemed eons ago.

"Rose," Grace said, "don't you want me to come?"

"Of course. Mom's been asking about you. Come on up and bring us some holiday cheer."

"I'll be there in an hour."

It was just about an hour after Grace's call that the telephone rang. Rose answered, half wanting it to be Daniel, half expecting it to be Grace with an excuse. It was a voice from the bottom of a well.

"Too bad you never come out to play."

"Who is this?"

"I have someone else to play with now. I have your little friend."

"What?"

"The little bumblebee."

Rose went cold. Don't worry, he's only bluffing. Be casual, don't give anything away. "I don't know what you're talking about."

"The one who wears the bumblebee jacket," he said. Grace's yellow jacket with the black hash marks, her black hair spilling across the shoulders.

This was the moment when the police should be tracing the call, closing in, catching the killer. But they hadn't installed the equipment yet, and there had been a pervading feeling that these were only crank calls. The killer's M.O., as Chief Henning called it, was to stalk his victims by car, not by phone.

Rose held the receiver in her sweaty hand while he supplied the graphic details. "Steel into flesh, like a warm knife into butter. I am going to eat her up, bite off that little nose, suck out those little eyes, chew on her rosy tongue."

Rose listened, knowing, this is *him*. I have heard those words before. I have been in that dark place, I have seen and felt what he is saying.

Revulsion overwhelmed her. She found her voice. "Why her? Don't hurt her. Let her go!"

The phone was dead.

Mom came running into the hall, Jerram came running out of his room, both of them shouting, "What's the matter, Rose?"

"The killer," she said, "the police . . ." At that moment the front doorbell rang. It was *him*. Rose shrank back. He had finished with Grace and had come for her.

Mom opened the door as Rose screamed for her not to.

"Hi! Merry Christmas everybody!" Grace said with a big smile. Behind her stood Gregory Paschek, grinning like an uncomfortable monkey. Their smiles slowly faded.

Mom regained her composure first. "Merry Christmas, dear. Rose isn't feeling so well right now."

"I'm feeling fine," Rose said shakily. It had all been a dirty trick.

"You don't look so fine," Grace said. Gregory nodded in agreement.

"Come in and have some eggnog," Mom said. Rose rushed up the stairs to the bathroom to throw up.

She told Silver Henning and Detective O'Hara what had happened. He had been out there, on their street, watching. Silver said he'd probably used the pay phone outside the Daycare Center building at the bottom of Franklin Street. It would have taken less than a minute to drive down there after spotting Grace.

"This sicko is enjoying himself," O'Hara said.

"Isn't it about time you did something?" Dad said.

"We're trying, Mr. Potter."

"Trying isn't good enough. This time it was a sick joke. Next time . . ." He left the words hanging.

But Silver said they had made progress. There was a connection now between a blue car and some stains found at Mrs. Wollenschaft's house in Westley. They had been rust stains after all, but in checking, the police had found some traces of human blood in the basement drains. Mrs. Wollenschaft's tenant had a blue car. But he was away somewhere and not available for questioning.

"We don't know if he's involved," O'Hara said. "He's been living there for years. A perfect tenant, no noise, no guests. Travels a lot."

"But human blood . . ." Mom said with a shiver.

"People do cut themselves shaving," said O'Hara. "We have to work with concrete evidence, Mrs. Potter. Facts."

"The facts are that this maniac was right outside our door, and the police did nothing about it."

"*If* it was the same man," O'Hara said. "In a case like this you get a lot of jokers. Could just have been someone making a crank call."

Dad looked disgusted. Jerram began a long story about a television program he'd seen, where the police ignored the warnings and the victim ended up dead.

O'Hara ignored that. "Rose, think hard, are you sure you didn't recognize the man's voice?"

It was impossible to know if it was the same voice as the man in the blue car, or Wallace Romola or anybody else she knew. Nancy and Cyn and Carla had said it was a face she'd recognize. But what face? All she knew was that she had been inside his mind, and she wasn't going to tell the police that.

She had to think harder, arrange and rearrange it because it was like an anagram.

The police would come to hook up their computers now. Chief Henning told them to answer all calls, try to act normal.

"Normal," Dad said with sarcasm.

But the only option was to do just that, act normal, as if nothing were happening. The alternative was to stay inside and worry. Rose knew she had to go to Muriel's to practice on Wednesday. For once, Mom agreed although she insisted on driving her down. Rose didn't argue. She didn't want a hassle. Just to get out of the house. Maybe get out of Bethboro.

As they came around the town common, they found themselves looking for Wallace.

"It couldn't be him, Mom."

"Of course not."

But their minds had been contaminated.

"Isn't that him over there?" Mom asked. "Hiding in those bushes?"

Rose couldn't see, but she wouldn't be surprised. Wallace liked to hide and jump out to scare people sometimes. Maybe she ought to admit it: Wallace wasn't responsible. He could be capable of . . . doing things.

"If you see him, don't talk to him," Mom cautioned. Mom dropped Rose off in front of the studio door.

"Maybe I should go up with you, to be sure she's here," Mom said.

"It's okay, there's her car." Rose pointed to Muriel's red Toyota at one of the parking meters in front of Robando's Real Estate.

Mom made Rose promise to call if Muriel couldn't give her a ride back home even though they'd been through it all earlier that morning, when Mom had phoned Muriel at her house to doublecheck everything. Even so, now she waited, the car spouting fumes into the cold air, until Rose had actually opened the door. Only when she was walking up the flight of stairs did Mom drive off.

Muriel must have just come in. She was sitting at her desk with her back to the door, still wrapped in her big cloak and talking on the phone. She raised a hand in greeting and made signals toward the locker room.

"I'll get changed," Rose whispered and hurried through to the lockers. The changing room had once been the apartment's kitchen and bath, and Muriel had kept the quaint old doors which were half smoked glass. Whenever they had the occasional male student, the younger girls would giggle and screech if they thought he was nearby, worried he could see through the glass.

She dumped her bag down on the bench and took off her parka.

There was always a faint smell of sweat in the room, something she would forever associate with dancing and sore toes.

She was pulling on her tights when Muriel came to the door. "Hi," Rose called, "I'll be ready in a minute."

Muriel didn't answer. Her shadow lingered for a moment at the glass, then disappeared. Out in the studio, the music began. Vivaldi. *Il Sospetto.*

Rose felt a tingle of excitement. A chance to dance for someone from New York at the recital. Lately, things had been getting in the way of dance. Now her resolve returned full force.

Muriel's shape reappeared. "Just coming," Rose shouted above the music.

But something.

Muriel's shadow remained. She was just standing there on the other side of the door, saying nothing. As if she were staring in. But Rose knew you couldn't really see anything, even if you felt like you could. That's what made the girls screech.

The feeling they were being watched.

"Muriel?"

Rose took a step to the door, half laughing. Then stopped. "Muriel? Is that you?"

Why was she joking around?

But the shape. Something was wrong. It was too tall. It suddenly seemed huge and black and menacing. And as Rose began to back away, two long arms went up and the hands splayed out against the glass. The shape was like a huge face now, the hands the two eyes, the spread fingers the eyelashes, the torso the long nose, and the edge of the glass like a thin-lipped mouth.

"Muriel, say something, okay?"

There was the faintest creak in answer. The door was slowly moving inwards.

Rose backed up fast, bumping into the bench, stumbling and running toward the bathroom. There was nowhere to go in there, just the sink and the stall and a tiny window high up.

Out in the locker room, the door banged. Footsteps. It couldn't be Muriel—she'd never do a thing like this. It was Christmas, not Halloween.

But even as Rose thought it couldn't be Muriel's idea of a joke, she was hoping it was. Her anger was rising, ready to be furious, praying to be furious with her.

There was only one place to hide in the room, a stupid useless place, a dead end. She went to it anyway, pushing at the stall door, a place to get into for shelter. The door moved inward an inch and stopped. She pushed harder but it wouldn't budge. Had Muriel stored the costumes in there? The footsteps were still coming, slow and regular, as if they wanted to provide time for panic.

Using the strength adrenalin was pumping into her veins, Rose pulled the door toward her instead. Please, please. With a great groan of stripped metal, the hinges turned backwards on themselves, and the door swung out.

Muriel was sitting on the toilet. She was wearing her black leotards and her paisley shawl. She was sitting very upright, her knees together, her hands folded primly in her lap. She seemed to be smiling. The faint scent of her expensive, spicy perfume mingled with the stronger, mordant smell of blood. Her throat had been cut from ear to ear.

"Hello, Rose," a voice said from behind.

Twenty-seven

IT WAS MURIEL DEAD AND MURIEL ALIVE AT THE same time.

But, of course not, no, the jaw was more square, showed the bluish tinge of a beard. The eyes were glittery, weird, maniac eyes.

"Surprise!" he said.

"You're twins."

"You should know all about that, Rose. Are we one, or are we two? Does one live for the other or by the other, or perhaps *in spite* of the other?" His glittery eyes darted about, came to rest on Muriel's body. He frowned. "Come away, let's close the door on that."

"I didn't know Muriel had a brother," she managed to say, knowing from somewhere deep within her that it was important to keep talking in a normal way. But her voice shook.

"Little Rose is scared."

"I'm not scared."

"Yes, you are!" His voice was churlish, as if he needed her to be scared. Was that how his victims had behaved? If she acted afraid would she die . . . or live? No way was he going to get her to grovel. She thought: I'll just turn around and walk out of here. Let him try to stop me.

His hand came out like a claw and pulled her back.

"Let's talk," he said. "I feel close to you."

Fighting revulsion at his touch, she was dragged into the small office. Here she and Muriel had talked of families. Muriel had cried about her own twin brother as Rose had told her about Jerram.

"We won't be disturbed." He turned the Vivaldi tape off and made her sit down. "Let's have a nice chat. Want some tea? No, don't want you upchucking your guts all over the place. I've been watching you, Rose. I found out all about you from . . . her." He jerked his head toward the dressing room. "I think you understand me, Rose. You're smarter than the others." He paused. "Why are you looking at your watch?"

She had been about to pretend that her mother was picking her up but realized he wouldn't believe it would be so soon.

"Someone is coming here," she said, getting a better idea, forcing her voice to stop quaking.

"No one is coming."

"Oh, yes. I'm auditioning today, for a company in New York. The director is coming to see me. He should be here any minute." She checked her watch again.

He smiled, and it was like watching an oil slick spread across the surface of a scummy sea. The smile leaked across his skin, turning his face into an evil clown's head. "A man from New York?"

Rose nodded, trying to look positive.

He sneered. "I'm the man from New York. Didn't you figure that out? Iver Westa, once a big name in dance." He jumped up and spun around in the small space, Muriel's cloak flying out like wings. *"Pas de bourrée? Entrechat?* I still have connections. Still useful. She told me all about you. Thought you could go places. Asked me to do her a favor." He smiled wickedly. "I bet that stuck in her craw! She ran away from me. Thought she could hide in this silly town. She never knew I was always close by; she thought I was still in New York." He looked smug. "I'm clever, a good watcher. Lived a double life. Pretended I was being a good boy. Told her I wanted to make up with her. Gave her my Christmas present. Told her how wrong she was about me." He sighed. "I think in the end, she saw the light."

Abruptly he sat down again and put his face close to Rose. "I have a present for you, too." He smelled of Muriel's perfume, but his breath was sour. She pulled back before she could stop herself.

He frowned. "Don't you want to see it?" The oil slick smile came back. "Of course you do."

He put his hand inside the cloak. What was he going to show her? Slowly he drew it out again. There, as glittery and keen as his eyes, was a big chef's knife.

"Blood is beautiful, don't you think?"

"No!"

"Scared now?"

"I don't think blood is beautiful. Why should it be?"

"Why not? We live with blood. We're full of blood. You're a walking blood bag. Did you ever think of that?" Her mind raced with what to say, to get him off the subject of blood.

"When you put the knife in," he went on and stuck the point of the blade against his thumb, "the blood blooms." A dark bead of blood appeared on the end of his finger. He licked it off. "Like a flower," he said, enraptured. "Want a taste?"

Again, she turned away. It upset him. He grabbed her chin and made her look at him. "Scared now?"

"No," she managed to say shakily.

Suddenly he let her go, seemed to lose interest, began haphazardly touching papers on Muriel's desk. "All my efforts were wasted in this town. I left clues but the idiots never understood them." He looked back at Rose. "Westa, you know? That's our name. The town I found to live in, Westley, that was a good clue. And my mark in the sealing wax. Red as blood, the imprint of a dancer's foot with a perfect arch. But they wouldn't print it in the newspaper." He was suddenly sullen. "Christmas is a bad time. I have to do certain things to make the pain go away. Certain things with girls. It helps." His smile was surprisingly artless, boyish now. "Perhaps you understand. But she . . . " He gestured again toward the dressing room. "She was always against me." He gave himself a shake and his expression changed. A crazy look in the eyes.

He waved the knife in front of Rose. "When you put the knife in, blood blooms like a flower.

Goes in soft like a knife through . . . "

She had been in his mind. She knew. " . . . butter," she finished for him. "Like jam on a sliced open bun."

It was gratifying to see him jump like a startled rabbit.

"Scared now?" she said.

But it lasted only a second and she realized he might be even more dangerous than before. Yet he looked at her with new interest. Could she get him to trust her . . . or to fear her?

"Little pumpkin," he said, sticking his face right into hers and smacking his lips so near that she tasted his spit.

She spit back in disgust instinctively; a bad move, his reaction was fierce. He leapt up again and began wiping his face with the cloak, his sleeve, some paper he grabbed from the desk.

"Dirty bitch," he screamed. "I'll get you for that."

He raised the knife, and she waited for it to come down into her. Thinking: Knives are more hideous than guns; the sight of the blade makes your skin crawl, you can't push a knife away because it eats your flesh, it is indeed like going through butter.

He lowered his arm. Looked her over, eyes narrowed, as if changing his mind. The silence was worse than the threat of the knife. She needed to fill it.

"Why'd you kill Muriel?" she asked.

His voice was petulant. "I *told* you. She blamed me for the puppy. I never did it. I was scared in the cellar. I cried and cried. But she wouldn't believe it. And she began to suspect . . . things. That's why she ran away. Then just when I thought it was all right, she changed her mind, she got mad again. She threatened to tell on me." He licked his lips nervously. "Women have power, don't they?" he asked.

Rose stared straight into his eyes. "Yes."

He looked away. I've got him, she thought triumphantly. It was so easy, he was just crazy, he was a little like Wallace, they couldn't concentrate on anything . . . they . . .

"I'm going to kill you right now," he said. With one hand he pressed her back against the chair. She was astonished at his strength. "You talk too much. Like the other one. I had to shut her up. Sometimes they were quiet and I could make it slow, so that the blood ran in beautiful rivers. But some talk and it must be fast."

Thank God it would be fast, Rose thought, not the slow, painstaking death.

"But I like you. It would be better slow." He pressed the cold blade against her throat. It tickled at first, and she had a horrible thrillish desire to laugh and scream *No, don't do it!* and then he pressed harder, and she could feel death against her flesh and it made her gag.

"Scared now?" he asked.

Slowly, he drew a red flower from beneath the cloak.

If she really had any power she could do something to stop him. I'm going to die, she thought. Well, it won't be so bad because it was lovely on the other side, but now at the hour of my death I feel like sticking around. Nancy, help me.

Somebody was breathing hard, Rose or him, it didn't matter, their breath was mixed up together. They could smell each other, feel each other, killing was a very intimate act. The river was running fast now. Their minds flowed together, thoughts and memories mixed. Rose felt a cold dark place, felt the tremors of a child's fear as it stared at a dead puppy. And he felt the long stretch of time that bound him to her, and he was angry. *Now,* he was thinking, I want it to be *now*. Suddenly Rose felt pain, saw the pinpricks of the stars, the rush of black space coming very fast as one of them lost consciousness.

"Many hurts I have had!" a voice cried, and a tap dancer's baton came crashing down on Iver's head.

"Many worries, many hurts," Wallace shouted as he brought the baton down again and again until Iver's face was crisscrossed with slashes and welts and blood did indeed bloom from his flesh.

"Stop, Wallace!" Rose screamed.

He looked at her, baton poised, then broke into tears. "Would I do that? No no no no."

"It's all right," she managed to say, her breath coming in painful gasps. "It was a good thing."

"Good?" he asked, bewildered yet happy. He took her hand. But she disengaged herself and stumbled to the phone, skirting Iver Westa's body and Wallace's sagged, sobbing figure. The phone was dead.

"We have to go outside for help, Wallace," she

said slowly, feeling herself still in the thick syrup of fear. Had to get out, away from *him*, from his eyes that were yet staring at her as if they could see into her soul. Was he dead? She didn't want to touch him to find out.

"Come on," she said to Wallace.

Wallace was looking down into the bloody face. "A trick of mirrors," he said. "Or a miracle."

Yes, Rose thought. That's why she almost recognized him in the car, why Nancy said it was a face she knew. The dark dancer.

She began to shiver violently, and Wallace was suddenly solicitous, taking off his dirty overcoat and wrapping it around her as they went down the stairs. She saw that he was shaking, too.

She took him into Robando's Real Estate office. At their entrance, everyone jumped up from their desks. But Rose saw in their hesitation, in the split seconds of wondering how to react, that they were fearful, of Wallace or perhaps even herself. She explained, slowly, her voice fading in and out, her tongue feeling numb.

Looking askance at them both, Lou Robando phoned the police. Reluctantly, he offered them coffee. "That's a nasty bruise on your neck," he said to Rose and stared at Wallace with suspicion.

Rose looked at Wallace gratefully. "He saved my life," she told Lou.

"Yeah? And how'd you happen to come along, buddy?" asked Lou.

"The girl told me," Wallace said.

"What girl? You mean Rose?"

"The girl in the white dress," Wallace said. "I don't know her name."

Lou Robando winked at Rose. "Sure thing."

Rose ignored Lou. Nancy had made one last visit, but she was unlikely to come back again. She patted Wallace's hand. A single tear slid down his cheek. She could feel her own tears starting to fall.

Jerram was the first to come rushing in, his face gray, his eyes sad.

"Are you okay, Rose?" He hugged her. "I didn't know you were in danger."

"That's because you're you and I'm me."

"And I never was anything like you, was I?"

"You're my brother, and I like you fine, just the way you are."

People were trying to push their way through the doors of the real estate office. Detective O'Hara, in a smart blue suit and gold chains, was giving orders to keep the gawkers out. She caught Rose's eye and gave her the thumbs up.

In spite of O'Hara, they came swarming in. Mom, Dad, reporters, more policeman. Finally, Daniel. That's when she saw Jerram slip away and walk off alone toward the common. She tried to reach him with the arms of her mind . . . just this once more.

Nothing.

But then he turned and stopped and looked back. He gave her a wave. Her heart lifted. See you later, Jerram, she thought. It was going to be all right now. No need to think about death anymore. The long seige of the Christmas Killer was over.

Part Eight

Him

PRISON IS NOT A BAD PLACE, NO WORSE THAN THE prison of my own soul. Here I am fed and clothed and cared for.

Oftentimes I think of her in the rides of night and wonder whereof she came. She is like me, not easily scared. Rose, my blood-red blossom, is alone worthy. One of these days I will make her my queen.

It is her *other* she must fight, not let him pull her down. He who is her brother can be a dangerous liability. Those who have never seen the heart of the beast cannot know the power. It may be someday she will have to end him as I ended she who was my sister.

In the meantime, I am waiting here. A place of between. Between death there is life. Between life there is death. It all adds up to the same thing.

Let a little time pass. I will send her a letter, tied up in my own blood and sealing wax. She will know me from my mark. And she will think of me again.

And, before long, I will escape from this place, and I will be seeing her again.

Patricia Windsor

The Sandman's Eyes £3.50

I have come back from being away a long time. My room is familiar, yet it feels as if it belongs to somebody else.

It's a cured me who sits in the kitchen this afternoon with Rosie and Grandfather. And I think: they don't know what to say to me. 'I have a job,' I say. 'I'm going to work up at the cemetery.' 'Oh Michael, you can't work in a graveyard.' 'Why not? It's a fitting position for a murderer.'

And the memories come flooding back: of the crumpled body that night in the park. After the man pushed her. The man they tried to say was me.

The Sandman's Eyes won the Edgar Allan Poe award from the Mystery Writers of America 1986.

All Pan Books are available at your local bookshop or newsagent, or can be ordered direct from the publisher. Indicate the number of copies required and fill in the form below.

Send to: Pan C. S. Dept
Macmillan Distribution Ltd
Houndmills Basingstoke RG21 2XS
or phone: 0256 29242, quoting title, author and Credit Card number.

Please enclose a remittance* to the value of the cover price plus £1.00 for the first book plus 50p per copy for each additional book ordered.

*Payment may be made in sterling by UK personal cheque, postal order, sterling draft or international money order, made payable to Pan Books Ltd.

Alternatively by Barclaycard/Access/Amex/Diners

Card No. | | | | | | | | | | | | | | | | |

Expiry Date | | | | | | |

____
Signature

Applicable only in the UK and BFPO addresses.

While every effort is made to keep prices low, it is sometimes necessary to increase prices at short notice. Pan Books reserve the right to show on covers and charge new retail prices which may differ from those advertised in the text or elsewhere.

NAME AND ADDRESS IN BLOCK LETTERS PLEASE

....

Name ______________________________

Address ______________________________

____

____

____

3/87